Have you got all the *Chestnut Hill* books?

Lauren Brooke

Chestnut Hill

Far and Away

■SCHOLASTIC

With special thanks to Elisabeth Faith

*For Johanna Penrose and Ben Bastion, with thanks for
your inspiration, and for Leila El-Said and your
endless enthusiasm. You make writing fun!*

First published in the UK in 2010 by Scholastic Children's Books
An imprint of Scholastic Ltd
Euston House, 24 Eversholt Street
London, NW1 1DB, UK
Registered office: Westfield Road, Southam, Warwickshire, CV47 0RA
SCHOLASTIC and associated logos are trademarks and/or
registered trademarks of Scholastic Inc.

Series created by Working Partners.

This edition published by Scholastic Ltd, 2013

Copyright © Working Partners, 2010

Cover photography © Equiscot Photography

ISBN 978 1407 13661 5

A CIP catalogue record for this book is available
from the British Library.

The right of Lauren Brooke to be identified as the author
of this work has been asserted by her.

Printed and bound by CPI Group (UK) Ltd, Croydon, CR0 4YY
Papers used by Scholastic Children's Books are made from wood grown in
sustainable forests.

1 3 5 7 9 10 8 6 4 2

www.scholastic.co.uk/zone

Two words drummed in time with Colorado's stride as the gelding trotted along the trail: *Honey's leaving, Honey's leaving.* Lani Hernandez had thought of nothing else since her best friend had made the shock announcement two days earlier. At any other time a Saturday morning trail ride with her three best friends would have filled Lani with joy. *But this is probably the last time the four of us will ride out together.*

Honey Harper pushed pretty grey Minnie level with Colorado. "Is everything OK, Lani?" Her blue eyes were worried. "You seem miles away."

About five thousand miles, Lani thought wryly. That was approximately how far away Honey would be once she relocated to Oxford in England. "I . . . I was trying to calculate a formula for how long it will take the maple trees to finish sprouting their new leaves." It was the first thing that came to mind but it was better than spoiling the ride for the others by admitting how upset she was feeling.

"Typical, Lani." Dylan Walsh looked back and

grinned. "Can't you ever give that brain of yours a break?"

"Mine is a lonely path to tread," Lani sighed, "destined to be misunderstood by the rest of society. Genius isn't something you can switch on and off, you know."

"In that case, you hide your suffering well," Dylan teased.

"Ah, see, a classic example of your misunderstanding," Lani fired back. "My genius doesn't ever switch off, but I do occasionally leave it on standby."

Malory O'Neil was riding abreast with Dylan. "I don't know about genius, but right now common sense is telling me that we should make the most of this stretch of grass with a canter. How about it, guys?"

Lani shortened her reins and felt Colorado bunch in anticipation. "Ready!" Ahead of them, the trail opened up into a grassy paddock with woodland at the far end. Within three strides Colorado had carried Lani past Honey and Dylan and was in determined pursuit of Malory on Tybalt. The dark brown gelding's long legs ate up the ground as Malory crouched over his neck, urging him to go faster.

"C'mon, Colly. We can take them!" Lani whooped. She stood in her stirrups to lighten her seat and felt Colorado open up his stride. Her hands became lost in his long mane as it flowed back in the breeze. Pushing her sadness to the back of her mind, Lani gave herself up to the thrill of the horses' hooves thudding over the soft turf.

Malory and Tybalt reached the field's boundary

fence seconds before Lani and Colorado. For one brief moment, Lani imagined setting Colorado at the post and rails. "And you'd clear it too," she murmured as she pulled him up. She looked pointedly at her watch as Dylan and Honey cantered up. "Did you guys stop for a cappuccino?"

"We were holding back to watch the two of you fight it out for first place," Dylan replied. She turned Morello and rode up to the five bar gate. As she bent down to open it, she glanced over her shoulder. "Who's going to be through first?"

Lani felt herself grin as Malory moved Tybalt to one side and gracefully, but cheekily, bowed at Lani. Lani nudged Colorado forwards and chuckled as they rode on to the woodland track.

Honey was the next to ride through. She halted Moonlight Minuet alongside Colorado and smiled as the beautiful grey reached out her nose to say hello to the dam pony. "Anyone would think they'd been apart for days, not minutes!"

"Hey, being apart for any length of time isn't easy when you're best buddies," Lani defended Colorado.

Honey winced and Lani suddenly realized what she'd said. *Way to go, Lani, you clutz.*

"No." Honey sounded flat. "It's not going to be easy at all." She looked down at her hands. "I keep on planning shopping trips and DVD nights and trail rides for next term, and then it hits me that I won't be around to do any of those things."

Lani reached over and squeezed Honey's arm. It

had been Honey's decision to go back home to England with her brother and parents but, if anything, that made it even more difficult for her. "No one blames you for wanting to be in the same country as your family," Lani said softly. "Yeah, sure, selfishly we all hoped you'd choose to stay here but that doesn't stop us understanding why you need to go."

Honey rubbed her hand across her eyes. "Don't set me off!" she pleaded, trying to laugh.

"Hey, didn't we make an executive decision not to mention Honey's grand departure during the ride?" Dylan demanded as she rode up with Malory. "Pretty soon we'll have her saying 'that's the last time I'll see that tree!'"

Lani was about to shoot her a caustic reply when she noticed that Dylan's green eyes looked suspiciously bright. "OK, folks." Lani forced herself to sound cheerful. They would not dissolve into mass tears! "We have a ride to enjoy."

"My sentiments exactly," Dylan agreed, swallowing hard.

They rode along the tree-lined path in silence. In the distance a bird flew out of a tree, sounding an alarm which made the ponies prick up their ears. All around them, branches were budding with new leaves and the air was filled with competing scents. Colorado snorted and shied as a baby rabbit burst out of the undergrowth. It narrowly missed his hooves as it skittered over the path. Lani shortened her reins and pushed him into a trot to give him something to think about. She rose and fell to his stride as they negotiated the twisting mud path that cut through the woodland. As they neared the end of the trail, the trees thinned out and tiny midges danced in the strong dappled sunlight. Lani reached the perimeter gate first and halted Colorado so she could pull back the clasp. Pushing open the gate, she waited for the others to ride through before closing it after them.

"So," Malory said as they left the woods behind, "has anyone got any exciting plans for Spring Break?" Her hand flew up to cover her mouth. "Oh my gosh! I can't believe I asked that."

"It's OK," Honey quickly assured her. "I'm flying back to England and staying with my Aunt Amy while my parents house-hunt. There, that's my plans over and done with. What about the rest of you guys?"

"Just the same old, same old." Dylan shrugged. "Two weeks at home missing you guys and Morello like mad." She reached forward to pat the skewbald gelding's neck.

"Lucky you," Lani sighed. "I'm not even leaving campus. My dad's made arrangements for me to stay at school as he's out of the country right now." Being a commander in the US Air Force meant that Lani's dad was often away.

"I could always ask my dad if you could come and stay with us," Malory offered. "He'll be at work so we'd have to entertain ourselves, and the flat's teeny. But if you don't mind sleeping on a camp bed I'm sure it will be fine for you to stay over."

"Thanks, Mal." Lani felt her spirits lift. It definitely

beat staying at school while all the other girls went home. "That would be ace."

As they rode over the brow of the hill they saw the campus spread out below them. Instinctively Lani knew that Honey would want a moment to take in the sight. She halted Colorado and the others pulled up next to her. Lani gazed down at Chestnut Hill's familiar red-brick buildings linked by winding pathways and lines of old-fashioned Victorian-style lamps. Beyond the dorms, the distant figures of grazing horses were dotted around the paddocks. Lani shot Honey a sideways glance. Her friend was sitting with her blue eyes stretched wide, drinking in every detail of the school campus as if she was trying to sear it in her memory.

"Let's go," Honey said abruptly. She closed her legs around Minnie and urged her forward.

Lani exchanged a glance with Dylan and Malory.

"This is so tough for her," Malory murmured.

And us, Lani thought unhappily. *Honey might be wondering how she's going to cope without life at Chestnut Hill, but how's life at Chestnut Hill going to be without her?*

Lani scooped up the last of her macaroni cheese. "I need to send some emails," she said, pushing back her chair. "I'll catch up with you guys later."

"Don't forget it's movie night," Malory reminded her.

Lani glanced at her watch. The Adams seventh- and

eighth-graders had agreed to meet in their shared common room at seven o'clock to put on a DVD. She had just half an hour before she needed to be over at Adams House. "I'll be there," she promised.

Threading her way through the cafeteria tables, Lani thought of the emails she needed to send. The first, to her dad, was straightforward. He was leaving the next day to fly overseas and she wanted to wish him a safe trip. The second email wasn't going to be as easy.

Sam, Lani thought as she headed into the computer suite. She didn't know how she was going to word the email to Honey's brother. She had been surprised that he hadn't contacted her already. She sighed. Sam was the reason why the news about the Harpers' relocation had come as a double blow. Lani had grown very close to Honey's twin brother since his recent battle with leukemia, and she knew that this was going to be an even harder goodbye.

Sitting in front of a spare monitor, she logged on. She dug her memory stick out of her bag and plugged it into the computer. Opening up a photo of herself, Malory, Dylan and Honey huddled together on the paddock fence she captioned it, *The Four Musketeers*. . . Attaching it to a brief chatty mail to her dad, she pressed send.

Now for the other email. Lani stared at the screen. For the first time in her relationship with Sam she was lost for words. He would be feeling bad enough about the relocation as it was without her making him feel worse.

Hey Sam,
When I said you'd never make the grade as an
honorary American until you quit calling soccer
football, I didn't expect you to hightail it back over
the Atlantic.

Lani paused and read back what she'd just typed. The tone was light and humorous, a world removed from what she felt. *Will he think I don't care?* With a groan she hit the delete button. Maybe this was one time when it was better not to email. *He's bound to call this weekend.* She logged off and pushed back her chair. *Maybe that's why he hasn't mailed. Better to talk this one through.*

As Lani made her way from the student centre to Adams House she wished she'd brought a jacket. Her thin Diesel T-shirt didn't have the barrier factor against the evening chill. Light spilled out of the Adams foyer windows and Lani welcomed the warmth as she walked inside.

In the far corner of the foyer, Honey was talking on the phone. She placed her hand over the receiver and mouthed, *"It's my mum."*

Lani nodded and pointed upwards. *"I'll see you upstairs,"* she mouthed back.

As she headed over to the curving staircase she heard her name called. Glancing over her shoulder, she saw Mrs Herson heading towards her carrying a tray of snacks.

"I thought you might enjoy these," the housemistress

explained with a smile. "I heard you were having a movie night."

Lani looked appreciatively at the popcorn, nachos, dips and fruit sticks.

"This is great, thanks!" she said, taking the tray. "Shall I send the others to see you for theirs?"

Mrs Herson's eyes twinkled. "Nice try but I'm not sure your relationship with Dylan could stand the strain if you deprived her of her favourite snacks."

Lani grinned. "I'd like to argue that I mean more to Dylan than a bowl of nachos but I'm not sure I have the confidence to put it to the test."

The corners of Mrs Herson's mouth tugged up. "Leave the tray in the common room. I'll collect it later when I come around for lights out."

Lani carefully carried the tray along the corridor to the common room. Inside the cosy room, the coffee table was already laden with bowls of crisps and cans of soft drinks. "Hey guys, make some room," Lani said. "Hersie's given a contribution."

Alexandra Cooper and Razina Jackson pushed the bowls closer together to clear a space. Lani set down the tray and then glanced around. "Since this is Honey's last Saturday night with us, how about we let her choose the DVD?"

The girls nodded, even Lynsey Harrison and Patience Duvall who could usually be relied on to object to anything Lani and her friends suggested.

"Where is she, anyway?" Dylan puffed as she helped to angle one of the sofas to face the wall-mounted screen.

"She's taking a phone call from her mom," Razina said before Lani had a chance to reply. "She went about ten minutes ago."

Lani went to the back of the room and collected a chair. As she added it to the curving row of furniture, she couldn't help noticing that Lynsey and Patience had bagged the most comfortable sofa placed right in front of the widescreen. *One, two* . . . she began to count, waiting for the inevitable eruption that would occur when Dylan noticed the pair's prime location.

She was distracted by Honey walking into the room. Her cheeks were flushed and her eyes shone brightly as she met Lani's quizzical gaze. *Oh my gosh, I bet her mum's told her they're not going to relocate after all.* Lani's heart leaped as she hurried over to Honey.

"What is it?" she asked.

Honey shook her head. "Wait for the others!" She beckoned to Malory and Dylan.

"You're not moving back to England?" Lani couldn't resist fishing.

Honey reached out and squeezed her hand. "I'm still going but. . ." she waited until Dylan and Malory had joined them, "so are you!"

Dylan looked from Honey to Lani. "So are we what?"

Honey's voice rose with excitement. "Coming to England! That's what my mum was calling about. She's already spoken with your parents about it and they've agreed. You're all flying over to England to spend Spring Break with us!"

Lani's heart skipped. "Please tell me you're not kidding."

"I'm not kidding," Honey promised, laughing. "As long as it's OK with you all, my parents will book tickets for you on our flight."

Lani let out a loud whoop. "This has got to be the most amazing news ever!"

"You're telling me!" Dylan exclaimed as she gave Honey a high five.

"I hate to cut in on your private happy party but some of us are waiting to watch the movie," Lynsey called over.

"And speaking of people you won't miss. . ." Lani murmured to Honey as they headed over to join the others.

Honey looked delighted to be in charge of the movie choice, and instantly picked one of their favourites, *Hidalgo*. No one had any complaints about watching Viggo Mortensen ride his brave Arabian mare on a long and perilous journey one more time. Wei Lin Chang flicked off the lights as the opening music blared out from the surround sound speakers. Lani stared at the screen but barely registered what was happening. All that kept running through her mind was Honey's news. *I don't have to say goodbye on Saturday.* She felt a rush of excitement. *I'll be going with her and Sam!*

As the closing credits came up on the screen Lani suggested to the others that they went to her and Honey's room to discuss the trip. Honey fished out her mobile from her pocket as they headed down the corridor. "I'm just texting my mum to tell her to go ahead and get your tickets. One of her friends works for the airline so we've got a special deal." She looked up at Lani. "Your mum was insistent that she'd pay for your ticket, but my dad persuaded her that this is our parting gift to you for putting up with me for so long."

Lani rolled her eyes. "Well, it's been quite a trial. . ."

"I can't believe this is happening." Malory shook her head. "England!"

"Land of mist and rain," Dylan said.

"That's Ireland." Honey giggled as she pushed open the door to the room.

Honey's side of the room looked depressingly empty. She'd taken down her horse posters and her timetable, and most of her other belongings were already in boxes. Lani sat down on Honey's bed and picked up Woozle, Honey's small brown bear. "So," she prompted, hugging the teddy, "tell us what Oxford's like."

"Very English," Honey replied with a grin. "It's a mix

of ancient and modern. Beautiful old buildings made out of stone that sometimes looks white, and other times golden or pink depending on the light. It's got a huge shopping centre and markets and fairs and theatres and a river. . ." She trailed off. "I can't wait to show you around!"

"It sounds amazing," Malory said. "And we're actually going to be there in just a few days!"

"We'll be staying with my Aunt Amy," Honey said. "I think I might have a photo of her somewhere." She opened the top drawer in her bedside cabinet and pulled out her photo album. She flicked through the pages until she came to a picture of a woman kneeling on a lawn with her arms around two golden retrievers. In the background was a handsome, wisteria-clad house that looked like a grand country hotel.

"This was taken about three years ago," Honey said, passing the album around.

Lani stared at Honey's aunt who was laughing up at the camera. A lock of curly blonde hair had fallen over her cheek. With her sparkling blue eyes and flushed cheeks she looked as if she had just finished playing an energetic game with the dogs. "She's younger than I expected," Lani commented.

"She's my mum's youngest sister," Honey said. "There's quite an age gap between them. Aunt Amy's in her late thirties."

"You look a lot like her," Dylan commented. "You've got the same heart-shaped face."

"She's great fun," Honey told them. "Sam and I

usually go to stay with her at least once a year. I'll never forget her coming into my room at midnight a few years ago. She got Sam and me to put on our Wellingtons and an overcoat and took us out into the woods behind her house. We went to a badger set and after a while a family of badgers came out and played in the moonlight. The babies were so adorable!"

Lani picked up on the warmth in Honey's voice. Her closeness to her entire family was obvious. It was no surprise that Honey couldn't bear the thought of the Atlantic Ocean separating her from them if she had decided to stay at Chestnut Hill.

"So what sort of daytime stuff do you get up to when you stay there?" Dylan asked as she passed the photo album to Malory.

"There's a racing yard about a mile away from the house," Honey said. "I sometimes hang out there and go up to watch the gallops."

"This just keeps getting better and better," Lani said. "We won't want to come back!"

"Maybe we can all find a boarding school to go to in England," Dylan said. "That way you'll never be rid of us," she told Honey.

Honey sighed. "I wish."

The door opened and Mrs Herson looked in. "Lights out in five minutes, girls."

Malory and Dylan got up. "See you in the morning." Malory handed the photo album back to Honey.

Lani waited for them to go before asking Honey a little shyly, "Will Sam be staying at your aunt's, too?"

"I think so," Honey said. "I know he's had a few invites from friends but I can think of one very good reason why he'll be turning them down." She raised her eyebrows questioningly.

Lani felt her cheeks grow warm. "I won't pretend I'm not glad to put off saying goodbye to him," she admitted.

"He'll miss you too," Honey said softly.

Lani looked down at her hands. "I never thought I'd find a boy who could get past the fact that I could whip him at baseball. I've always been treated as one of the guys. Sam's the first to see something else there."

She glanced up and met Honey's unwavering gaze. "You're not thinking of ditching your friendship with me, are you?" Honey asked unexpectedly.

"You know I'm not!" Lani protested.

"Well, it's the same with Sam," Honey said. "I know that you're not going to be able to meet up for dates any more, but that doesn't mean your friendship with him has to be over."

Thoughtfully, Lani padded over to her own bed and pulled out her pyjamas from under the pillow. She'd been so focused on having to break up with Sam that she hadn't considered an alternative. *But Honey's right. Our friendship is for ever, so why can't it be the same for Sam and me?*

Curling up in bed, she kept imagining how amazing Spring Break was going to be. *Roll on next Saturday!*

*

"I don't get how you can keep working at every lesson, Hon," Dylan commented as the girls carried their trays over to their table. She held up her hand and began to count off all the reasons why Honey should be cutting herself some slack. "One," she said, striking her little finger, "it's a Monday when no one should be up to full speed. Two, it's the week before Spring Break and everyone knows that's the time to start winding down, and three," she jabbed her middle finger, "the teachers would all turn a blind eye to you not getting any work done at all since they know this is your last week!"

"But I like working in class," Honey told her. She forked up a mouthful of salad. "If I didn't get on with my work I'd be really bored."

Dylan shook her head. "You're a lost cause, Felicity Harper."

Malory tore open her sachet of ketchup. "How about in our next class? Is Honey still supposed to slack?"

"Riding is one class where I can agree that working hard is fun," Dylan said. She picked up her chicken wrap and prepared to take a bite out of it. "Unless it involves riding without stirrups, that is."

Lani didn't mind riding Colorado without stirrups, although she would prefer to use her Western saddle for that particular exercise. "Wouldn't it be great if we could fly the horses over to England with us?" she mused.

"Could you imagine them all sitting in a row watching the in-flight movie?" Dylan said with a burst of laughter. "Morello would definitely want to watch

Hidalgo. With his colouring he might well be Hidalgo's great-great-great-great-grandson!"

"Tybalt would want *Seabiscuit*," Malory said. "A horse who, against all the odds, wins through."

Lani glanced at Honey and saw a sad expression flit across her face. *It's OK for us, we're only being separated from the horses for a couple of weeks. Honey's leaving Minnie behind for good.* Kicking herself for bringing up the topic, she tried to think of a change of subject. "Can you believe Mrs Von Beyer set a test today?"

It had the desired effect. Dylan gave a dramatic groan. "Hasn't anyone told her it's the week before vacation? Who wants to spend the whole of prep tonight swotting up History?"

"You have a hard life," Malory said, her mouth tugging up at the corners.

"Tell me something I don't know," Dylan said. "It's only being able to whinge to you guys and Morello that keeps me out of professional therapy!" She pushed back her chair. "Are you guys ready to hit the stables?"

Lani scooped up the last of her chilli. "Now that's a question you never have to ask!"

Lani trotted Colorado into the indoor arena and was surprised to see that the sand was bare. Usually Ali Carmichael, the director of riding, would have jumps already set out. Lani joined on to the end of the line of riders and began to rise in time with Colorado's stride. Colorado mouthed the bit playfully but when Lani closed her legs he settled into a steady, rhythmic pace. Lani glanced across the arena and watched Honey working Minnie in a collected canter. *They make such a perfect combination.* Honey rode elegantly and totally complemented Minnie's graceful movements.

Lani's attention was suddenly brought back home when Lynsey turned in her saddle and snapped, "Do I need to hang a sign on Quest's tail saying *'back off'*?"

Lani closed her fingers on the reins and lengthened the distance between Colorado and Quest. *Good thing it wasn't Bluegrass*, she thought. Lynsey's own pony, who was still recovering from a leg injury, was more protective of his personal space than Quest.

"OK, class, come and line up." Ms Carmichael waved them into the middle of the arena.

Lani halted Colorado alongside Malory. Tybalt shook his head impatiently, making his black mane bounce against his neck. "He never likes the standing part," Malory said ruefully. She gave Tybalt's shoulder a gentle pat. "Steady, boy."

Ali Carmichael waited for everyone to line up before announcing, "I've decided that we're going to suspend our module on equitation for this week. I'm setting you a new task instead. I'm going to put you into two groups and I want you to choreograph a routine to music which you'll demonstrate for me at the end of the week."

Lynsey groaned. "I can't believe we're abandoning equitation for more ballet! Haven't we had enough of dancing horses already?"

"I thought you were all due a bit of fun to mark the last week of term," Ms Carmichael said. She smiled at

Honey. "And I thought it would be an enjoyable way for you to end your time with us."

Good for Ms C, Lani thought, knowing that working with Minnie to music headed Honey's list of favourite equestrian activities.

"Lynsey, Honey, Lani, Dylan, Malory and Tessa, you're in group one, headed up by Honey," Ms Carmichael announced. "You can practise here. The rest of you need to ride down to the outdoor arena. Ms Phillips is waiting for you down there."

Ms Carmichael waited for them to ride out of the arena before she turned to Honey's group. "I'm going to play your soundtrack for you now. Listen to it a few times before you work out your floor plan. If any executive decisions need to be made then they're Honey's call."

Lani tried to hide a grin at the mutinous expression on Lynsey's face. As music sounded over the PA system, Lynsey said, "What is *that*?"

"It's the Beatles." Honey tipped back her head and laughed. "Brilliant!"

They listened to the medley of songs twice before beginning to plan their routine.

"We could start in the middle of the arena and canter out to the edges like an exploding star," Dylan suggested.

Honey nodded. "Good call."

"That could be our theme," Malory mused. "Joining and parting." She smiled at Honey.

"How about we ride the first move now and then

come up with other suggestions as we go along?" Lynsey said as Quest pawed impatiently at the ground.

"OK," Honey agreed.

Lani turned Colorado and squeezed her legs to get him to rein back into position. Colorado flattened his ears and swung his quarters out at Morello. "I know this doesn't make any sense but trust me, OK?" Lani murmured. She used her leg behind the girth to straighten Colorado before asking him to rein back again.

"Ready?" Honey called. "Go!"

Lani used her legs strongly and Colorado snorted with surprise. He gave a strong push with his hindquarters and cantered down the diagonal. As they reached the far corner of the school Lani used her legs again and closed her fingers on the reins to bring Colorado to a rather ragged stop.

He thinks I've gone mad, she thought as Colorado's ears flashed back again.

"I think we should turn and canter on the left rein for a circuit," Lynsey called out.

"How about we then alter the distances between us so that three of us are riding one side and three of us the other? We can halt and swap sides of the arena in time to the beat," Tessa suggested.

"OK, let's take it from the top," Honey called.

Lani turned Colorado and trotted him back to the centre of the arena.

"I don't know how many times I'll be able to get Tybalt to do this before he pitches me into the sand,"

Malory commented as Tybalt refused to rein back into position.

Lynsey rolled her eyes. "And Ms Carmichael thinks we'll be ready to go with this by the end of the week? Some hope!"

"I have every confidence in you," their instructor called back from the judges' box where she was operating the stereo system.

"Me too," Honey chipped in. "Come on, guys, we can do this!"

Lani dissolved into giggles as Tybalt finally backed into the centre and sprang into a canter without waiting for Malory's signal. "Maybe we should choreograph something less complicated."

"One last try," Honey said. She waited for Malory to persuade Tybalt back into position before saying, "Go!"

Lani pushed Colorado into a canter and as they neared the corner of the arena she prepared him to turn left. Keeping an eye on the others, she closed the gap between herself and Tybalt as they cantered a circuit.

"Halt!" Lynsey called when she, Dylan and Tessa were directly opposite Honey, Malory and Lani.

Lani squeezed her rein and obediently Colorado gave a quarter turn and came to a neat stop.

"Now swap sides," Lynsey called. "Working trot!"

Lani half-halted to keep Colorado at the same pace as Tybalt and Minnie. She flashed Dylan a grin as they passed each other in the centre of the arena.

As they reached the other side Dylan let out a whoop. "We totally rock!"

Honey laughed. "With the soundtrack we've got, we'd better!"

Lani patted Colorado's neck. "So guys," she called, "what's next?"

They spent the next half hour working and reworking their steps. For the final movement they rode into the centre with Honey in the middle. Lani, Honey and Malory faced forwards with Dylan, Tessa and Lynsey facing the opposite direction. "One, two, three," Dylan counted. In time to the music they rode the horses forward in concentric circles, forming a cartwheel movement.

Lani glanced at Honey. *I can't imagine what it will be like without her in the centre of everything.* She felt a surge of sadness. *Life at Chestnut Hill is never going to be the same again.*

Lani unbuckled Colorado's girth and lifted off his saddle. Steam rose up from his damp coat. Lani dipped a sponge into a bucket of water and began washing Colorado down. Taking a face sponge, she wiped carefully around his eyes and nostrils before drying him off. As she turned to lift Colorado's rug off the half wall she felt his nose bump her shoulder. A moment later he began pretending to chew her hair.

"Is that a heavy hint that it's dinner time?" Lani joked. "Hold still while I put on your rug and then I'll see what I can find you."

She buckled the rug under his belly before heading down to the feed room. There was an open sack of carrots in the corner of the room so Lani took a handful. Colorado was looking over his door expectantly. When he saw Lani he raised his head and gave a drawn-out whicker.

"Here you are, hungry boy." Lani snapped a carrot into small pieces and fed them to him one by one. Once Colorado had finished, Lani went to Morello's stall. "I thought he might like a treat." She held out another carrot to Dylan.

"For his performance?" Dylan pulled a face. "It was the equivalent of dancing *Swan Lake* in a pair of Wellingtons." Grudgingly she began to break up the carrot. "You so do not deserve this," she admonished Morello as he stretched out his nose to sniff at her hand.

Lani grinned. Morello had been fine right up until he was asked to try a flying change at canter. No amount of cajoling or bribery from Dylan had persuaded him to co-operate. Leaving them to it, Lani headed to Minnie's stall. Looking over the wall, she thought for a moment that the grey mare was alone and guessed that Honey had already finished up. But before she held out the carrot, Lani heard a muffled sob. Leaning over the wall, she saw Honey standing on the far side of Minnie with her head pressed against the mare's neck. Lani hesitated, torn between going in to comfort her friend and leaving her to cry it out with Minnie. Her hand hovered over the bolt on the door.

"Oh Min, I don't want to leave you," Honey murmured.

Lani's hand dropped down to her side. She turned and walked quietly away, her heart heavy. This wasn't her moment, it was Honey's and Minnie's – and one of the last ones they had left. Lani couldn't deny them that.

3

"Lani." A voice spoke insistently. "It's time to wake up!"

Lani opened one eye a fraction. "Are you crazy? It's still dark."

"I know." Honey's voice was full of laughter. "OK, I'll leave you to sleep. I guess I'll just have to send you a postcard from England."

Honey's words had the same effect as an upended jug of ice-cold water. "I'm up!" Lani kicked off her duvet and groped around for her dressing gown. She yelped as she stubbed her toe against the suitcase at the end of her bed.

"Stay still," Honey commanded. A moment later light flooded the room.

"Wattage overload!" Lani pressed her arm over her eyes.

Honey snapped off the overhead light and switched Lani's bedside light on instead. "Better?"

"Much." Lani blinked as her eyes adjusted. She felt a rush of excitement. "This time tomorrow I'm going to be waking up in England!"

"This time tomorrow it will be mid-morning in England," Honey pointed out. "Unless we miss our flight, that is."

Lani took the hint. Gathering up the clothes she'd laid out the night before, she sprinted for the bathroom door.

She washed and changed at lightning speed and ran through her mind everything she needed to have with her when they left. *Passport, clothes, mobile, chargers*, she thought as she walked back into the bedroom. She was distracted by a soft knock at the door. Mrs Herson looked in. "I thought you might like some hot chocolate." She held out a tray on which were two mugs and a pile of buttered toast.

"Do you think Mr Herson would miss you if you came over to England with us?" Lani said as she took the tray. "I sure could get used to this kind of treatment."

"I fully intend to have a vacation once you're gone," Mrs Herson told her, "which hopefully will involve Mr Herson bringing me my own tray of breakfast." She glanced at Honey. "Your parents will be here soon to pick you up. Can you be down in the foyer in ten minutes?"

Honey nodded. "Sure."

Lani bit into her toast as their housemother left the room. "Your aunt doesn't happen to employ a butler, does she? If Hersie can't come and serve us breakfast every morning then I'll settle for butler service."

Honey laughed. "We'll see what we can do!" She pulled out each of her bedside drawers and dropped to her knees to check under her bed. "I think I've got everything."

"You've forgotten the photo of you and Minnie." Lani pointed to the framed picture of Honey sitting on the paddock gate with her arm draped over Minnie's neck.

Honey shook her head. "I've got plenty. I wanted you to have this one." Picking up the photo, she handed it to Lani. "Here, something for you to remember me by."

"Did you think I'd forget you that quickly? As if!" Lani forced her tone to be jovial. She set the frame down on her own bedside table and turned away before her eyes started getting damp.

"Come on," she said as she shouldered her giant holdall. "We've got a plane to catch!"

Lani flashed her boarding pass to the flight attendant and followed Honey up the aisle to their row of seats. "I left my magazine behind in the lounge," Dylan complained behind Lani. "I was halfway through completing the competition on dressage terms."

"I'm afraid there's no going back for it now," Mrs Harper called from two rows back where she and Mr Harper were sitting.

"They were offering a dressage saddle as first prize," Dylan said as she stowed her hand luggage. She stood back for Sam to go ahead of her and sit by Lani.

To Lani's surprise, Sam waved Dylan and Malory in first. "I get travel sick if I'm not on the end of the row," he explained.

Lani tried to push away her disappointment. Part of the excitement of the flight for her had been a chance to spend time with Sam.

Malory sat alongside Lani. Her blue eyes sparkled with excitement. "How amazing is this? I've never been on a plane before. Is it true you can get a drink whenever you want one?" Before Lani could stop her, Malory pressed the button to summon a flight attendant.

"Um, Mal. . ." Lani began.

A flight attendant came to the end of their row. "Is there a problem?"

"What drinks do you have, please?" Mal asked.

Lani pressed her hand over her mouth to muffle a snort of laughter. Malory glanced at her in confusion before smiling back at the attendant.

"We'll be bringing breakfast around once we're in the air," the attendant said a little frostily. "Now, if you don't mind, I need to finish boarding."

Malory's cheeks burned red as the others burst into laughter. "It's not my fault, the figure on the button is holding out a cup of tea," she said. "How was I supposed to know it wasn't for refreshments?"

"You weren't." Lani recovered herself. "Just don't go pressing anything else without checking with us first, OK?"

"I won't." Malory grinned as she saw the funny side. "I'm going to stay rooted for the entire flight."

Lani glanced across at Sam and tried to catch his eye. He fished his iPod out of his pocket and slipped his earphones in. "I don't know about you guys but I got hardly any sleep last night," he said with a yawn. Leaning back in his seat he closed his eyes.

Lani opened her book. The text blurred as she stared down until she was unable to read a single word. *I don't get him. Why doesn't he want to spend the flight talking to me? We've got hardly any time left together, we shouldn't be wasting it.* She sighed. It had to be because he was so tired. *He'll be fine after he's caught up on some shut-eye.* Pulling her eye mask over her eyes, she figured catching up on sleep was a good idea. *It's not like I intend wasting much time sleeping when I'm in England.* She was going to make every moment count, even if it meant staying awake twenty-four hours a day.

"There we are." Mr Harper strode into the arrivals hall ahead of the girls and pointed into the waiting crowd. On the other side of the barrier a uniformed man was holding up a sign which read *Harper*.

Lani swapped an excited glance with Dylan as they made their way outside. Their driver led them to a gleaming black minibus with tinted windows. Sliding back the door, he glanced at Mrs Harper. "Mind the step, madam, it's rather high."

"I thought people only said things like that in movies," Lani murmured as she followed the others on to the bus.

Honey gave a small, mysterious smile. "Maybe you are in a movie," she suggested playfully. "Yanks on tour in Merrie Olde Englande!"

Mrs Harper handed out apples and bags of crisps

after everyone had stashed their luggage. "A little something to keep you going until dinner tonight," she explained.

Lani opened the packet of Ready Salted, muttering, "*Crisps*, not chips, *crisps* not chips," under her breath. She was determined to learn as much British vocabulary as she could during her visit. "How many hours until we reach Oxford?" she asked as the minibus pulled away.

"Just over one," Honey told her.

Dylan looked surprised. "Is that all?"

Honey nodded. "We're not in the USA any more," she teased. "You can drive from one end of the UK to another in about sixteen hours!"

"Say, are we going to be anywhere near Loch Ness? I'd love to go Nessie spotting." Dylan twisted in her seat to look at Sam who was in the seat behind.

"Sure," he said with a grin. "Maybe we could take a picnic and make a whole day of it."

Lani knew Sam well enough to know he was teasing. "Loch Ness is in Scotland," she told Dylan, "not England."

"And before you ask, no, we don't have any lochs or monsters in Oxford," Sam interjected.

Dylan screwed up her empty crisp packet and tossed it at Sam who ducked. "OK, so the G for gullible has just dropped off my forehead," she told him. "So don't try going there any more."

"Are there any castles near your aunt's home?" Malory asked. "I'd love to see one."

"There's Oxford Castle," Honey told her. "It was built

in the eleventh century, not long before the first colleges opened."

Malory shook her head, making her dark curly hair fall softly against her cheeks. "I can't believe we're going to be so close to all that history."

"Spoken like a true American tourist," Dylan teased.

"Nothing wrong with that." Mr Harper shrugged off his jacket and draped it over the back of his seat. "It's tourism that helps sustain the UK economy."

"Dad!" Honey groaned. "Can you take off your professor's cap? Chill! You're supposed to be on holiday!"

"Point taken." Mr Harper's eyes twinkled. He unfolded his newspaper. "Let's say the relaxing begins right now."

"Next he'll be quoting something out of Charles Dickens about empty vessels making the most noise," Sam said in a stage whisper. "He always does that when he wants us to be quiet."

"You'll have to change your tactics, Nigel," Mrs Harper warned. "It would seem that they're on to you."

Lani joined in the laughter, and thought, not for the first time, how charming Honey's family was. *It's going to be so great spending time with them.*

The sun was just beginning to dip below the horizon when the minibus turned off the main road.

"We're not too far away now," Mrs Harper announced.

As they travelled along the country lanes, all Lani

31

could see was miles and miles of green fields, divided by hedgerows.

"Oh my gosh, how cute is that?" Dylan exclaimed, pointing out of her window.

Lani leaned forward to look out of Dylan's side of the bus. They were passing a sugar-pink cottage with a golden thatched roof and cream roses climbing around the front door. A little further along stood a row of smaller white-painted cottages, set back from the road in long, narrow gardens full of tall flowers.

"Those are some of the estate cottages," Honey explained.

"Estate?" Lani raised her eyebrows. "What estate?"

"The Dysart estate," Mr Harper told her as the minibus pulled up in front of a pair of wrought-iron gates. The driver pressed a button on a small black plastic control and the gates began to swing open. "Welcome to your English home!" Mr Harper declared as the bus rolled forward again.

Lani frowned. "Er, what's your aunt's last name?" she asked Honey.

"Mason," Honey replied. "Until she got married, that is. Then she became Amy Dysart."

"No way!" Dylan sounded impressed. "Your aunt lives *here*? And the whole place is named after her husband?"

"Well, it's named after his family, really," said Honey, whose cheeks were starting to turn pink.

The minibus drove along a smooth curving road which had acres of parkland on each side stretching as far as the eye could see. They turned another bend and a huge red-brick house appeared in the distance. It was at least four storeys high, Lani guessed as she quickly counted windows, and the front door stood at the top of an elegant double-sweep of white stone steps.

"Someone pinch me." Dylan's eyes stretched even wider as she stared out of her window. "What is this, some sort of royal hunting lodge?"

Lani's mind went into overdrive. She had seen the house before, she knew she had. *It was in the photograph of Honey's aunt*, she realized. She had assumed it was a grand country hotel, not a private house! Lani shook her head. "Hey, Honey, why didn't you let on that you were nobility?" She spoke lightly although underneath she couldn't help feeling hurt that Honey had kept such major information from her.

"We're not," Honey said in a rush. "The only connection is through Aunt Amy's marriage."

"So we're going to be staying with aristocrats for Spring Break?" Dylan sighed and clasped her hands over her chest. "Will there be any eligible bachelors?"

"They're not like that at all." Honey laughed. "They're very down to earth, I swear."

The minibus crunched over clean brown and white gravel as it circled a low-walled pond and parked in front of the house. Lani blinked in disbelief. *I know I'm not dreaming, but if I was, this sure wouldn't be something I'd want to wake up from in a hurry.* She shouldered her bag before stepping off the bus, already planning to start taking photos as soon as possible. Her sisters were never going to believe her without hard evidence!

The double front doors were flung open and a woman wearing jeans and a padded sleeveless jacket over a threadbare sweater ran down the steps with her long blonde hair bouncing on her shoulders. "You're here, you're here! How was the flight?" she exclaimed as she hugged Mrs Harper followed by Honey's dad.

"Uneventful," Mrs Harper told her. She turned to the girls. "Meet Honey's Aunt Amy, everyone. Amy, meet Dylan, Lani and Malory."

Amy smiled widely at them as she tucked a piece of hair behind one ear. "Welcome to Dysart Hall. We're really looking forward to having you with us."

She sounds even more British than Honey, Lani thought as Amy threw her arms around Honey and Sam.

"It's so good to see you two!" Amy stood back and looked them up and down. "Sam, I'm sure you've grown at least three inches since as I saw you last."

Sam pushed his hand through his hair. "Maybe two and a half," he said, the corners of his mouth tugging up.

"We weren't sure if you would want a formal meal, so there are sandwiches and cake in the drawing room," Amy told them as a dark-haired man wearing an open-necked shirt and light brown trousers stepped out of the house. "Tom will take your luggage into the house."

"Another guest?" Dylan murmured hopefully to Honey.

"Staff, and very happily engaged to Sally, the

34

housekeeper." Honey's voice trembled with laughter as she linked arms with Dylan.

Tom shot them a friendly smile as he headed down to pick up their bags.

"Come in," Amy urged. Her eyes sparkled. "It's so wonderful to have you all here!"

Lani hesitated before she followed the others into the house. Turning around on the top step, she stared at the rolling green meadows dotted with trees. It was similar to Chestnut Hill, which had originally been modelled on an English country estate, but there was something different in the air – a cool softness that smelled of leaves and rain and earth. Lani imagined galloping Colorado over the grass, his hooves thudding sweetly on the turf. *Goodbye Chestnut Hill, hello Jane Austen*, she thought as she stepped into the entrance hall. Dominating the space was an ornate oak staircase leading up to a galleried landing. Half of the hall was oak panelled, and every inch of the walls was covered with heavy and rather forbidding gilt-framed oil paintings. A quick glance told Lani that most of them were of people in old-fashioned clothes, although one or two showed horses grazing under trees or prancing down to the start of a race.

Voices spilled from the room on Lani's right. Following the sound, she entered a room which was more welcoming than the hall, with cosy cream walls instead of oak panels. It was also one of the largest sitting-rooms Lani had ever seen; she counted three separate seating areas made up of an assortment of perfectly matched sofas and armchairs. Porcelain-based lamps standing on highly polished tables gave off a warm glow. A woman with sun-streaked hair was pulling huge drapes over the floor-to-ceiling windows. The ornate plasterwork on the ceiling caught Lani's attention. Moulded leaves and flowers picked out with delicate touches of gold paint encircled large round knots in the centre of the white-painted panels.

Dylan and Honey were talking to Honey's parents by the large stone hearth halfway along the room. Lani's eyes widened at the huge iron turning-spit that was suspended over the fireplace.

"No hog roast, I'm afraid," said Amy, walking over with a plate of thinly cut sandwiches, "but I can offer you an egg sandwich."

"Thanks." Lani took one even though she wasn't particularly hungry. A grandfather clock in the corner of the room revealed it was seven-thirty but she couldn't tell what time she felt like inside. She glanced at Sam and wondered when they'd be able to have a chance to hang out.

Sam was perched on the edge of a faded sofa. His eyes met hers briefly before he looked away.

Lani frowned. She wasn't imagining it; Sam was definitely avoiding her. *But why? Does he feel awkward because his folks are around?*

"Isn't this amazing?" Malory joined Lani balancing a plate in one hand and a glass of lemonade in the other. "I had a hard enough time getting my head around the fact we were in England. How am I ever going to get it to sink in that we're staying in an English manor house?"

Before Lani could reply, the panelled door opened and a woman with wavy snow-white hair walked into the room.

"They're here!" Amy called across to the older lady.

"My hearing may be fading but my eyesight's not," came the reply.

Amy laughed. "Lani, Malory, Dylan, this is my mother-in-law, Lady Margaret. She lives in the Dower House on the other side of the estate."

"Meg will do nicely," the old lady corrected her as she walked over to the sideboard to pour herself a cup of tea. She was dressed casually in a tweed waistcoat and linen trousers but she moved as if she was gliding across a dance floor.

"Are all of the rooms ready, Sally?" Amy asked the woman with sun-streaked hair.

Sally looked up from the hearth where she had started to build a fire. "Everything's good to go," she said cheerfully in a broad Australian accent, "and Tom's taken the cases up."

Desperate to get Sam to acknowledge her, Lani called over, "Where's your room, Sam?"

Without missing a beat Meg commented, "Young ladies are much more forward then they used to be in my day!" Her voice rang with amusement. She took a sip of her tea before walking over to the sofa. Sitting down, she added to Sam, "And a lot prettier, too." She gave Lani an approving mischievous look.

Lani felt herself turn bright red. She hoped Sam would bail her out but instead he got up and crossed the room to help Sally light the fire.

Putting her teacup down on the low table, Meg clasped her hands over her chest. "L'amour," she sighed. "It's such a wonderful thing, especially when you're young, eh, Sam?"

Sam shrugged his shoulders without turning around.

Lani's breath caught painfully in her throat. Across the room, Honey was staring at her twin, a frown creasing her brow.

Swiftly Dylan walked over to join Lani and Malory. "Just what is his problem?" she hissed.

Lani bit her lip as she watched Sam push logs on to the fire with more force than was needed. She didn't have a clue what was bugging him. *But one thing's for sure: I totally intend to find out.*

Sally pushed open a solid wooden door. "I've put you all in Meg's old room," she told the girls. "I thought you might like to be together."

Lani trooped behind the others into the large south-facing room. A four-poster bed stood against one wall with heavy tapestry curtains hanging from the dark wood frame. The duvet was pulled back to show a bolster dividing the mattress. On each side of the four-poster was a single bed. "In medieval times, this would have been a truckle bed." Sally nodded at the nearest single. "It would have been small enough for the Lady's maid to sleep on at night and be rolled back under the four-poster during the day."

"So I guess if I get to sleep up here, that makes the others my servants?" Dylan flopped down on one half of the four-poster.

Honey laughed. "Talk about having ideas above your station."

Sally pointed at a table. "There are some freshly baked chocolate-chip biscuits in the tupperware." She paused. "I guess I should call them cookies, not biscuits! There's also orange juice in the jug. If you need anything else just come and knock on my room, Honey knows which one it is."

The girls thanked her and as the housekeeper left, Lani caught sight of the carriage clock on the mantelpiece. "I can't believe it's nine o'clock. I'm nowhere near ready to go to sleep."

"It would only be four p.m. back in Virginia," Malory reminded her as she headed over to the far side of the room. Their bags had been put on an ottoman positioned between the two windows. Malory unzipped hers and pulled out her pyjamas.

"The bathroom's through that door." Honey pointed to a door opposite the beds.

Malory padded across the room. "Hey you guys, you've got to see this," she called.

Dylan scrambled off the bed and hurried into the blue and white tiled bathroom with Lani. A roll-top bath with claw feet stood in the middle of the floor. Opposite was a toilet complete with a cistern high on the wall and a long chain handle. The basin was enormous, almost large enough to be a bath itself, and the taps were made from old gleaming bronze.

"There's no shower so if you want to wash your hair you'll have to use the jug for rinsing," Honey explained from the bedroom. On the window ledge stood a blue floral jug in a matching basin. Sally had set out a pile of soft white bath towels and a wicker basket containing a collection of bubble bath, shampoo and soap.

"All we need now is someone to run the bath and it would be pitch perfect," Dylan commented.

Lani retraced her footsteps back into the bedroom. "Dylan needs bringing back to Earth. Any suggestions?"

"How about early mucking out duty?" Honey suggested.

There was an excited shriek from the bathroom and Dylan and Malory raced back into the room. "Did someone mention horses?" Dylan asked breathlessly.

Honey sat down in the window seat and hugged her knees against her chest. "Racehorses, to be exact," she said with a smile. "Remember I told you about hanging out on the gallops when I used to stay here? The estate's farm was converted into a racing yard nearly a hundred years ago. Meg's husband used to run it and hoped to pass it on to Uncle Timothy – that's Aunt Amy's husband – but he was more interested in working in the city."

Lani joined her on the window seat. "So who runs it now?"

"Uncle Timothy's cousin, Henry Stilling," Honey told them. "He's got a few really promising horses on the yard. I'll take you over to see them tomorrow."

Lani shook her head. "This is going to be the most amazing vacation ever!"

Honey reached over and squeezed her arm. "We're going to do our best to make sure it is." She glanced at her watch. "Who's first up to use the phone?"

"Well, I can use up some of my free minutes on my BlackBerry," Dylan replied, "and Mal's about to jump in the tub, so why don't you go first, Lani?"

Lani slipped down from the window seat. "I won't be long." She crossed the room, opened the door and hesitated.

"Left!" Honey called.

"Thanks for the heads up," Lani called back. "I'd have gone right!" She headed down the landing and turned the corner which brought her on to the galleried landing. Jogging down the staircase, she found her way to the library where Amy had said there was a phone.

Two of the walls were lined from ceiling to floor with books. *You could spend every day of your life reading and you wouldn't get through half of them*, Lani thought. She spotted the phone on the leather-topped desk in the middle of the room. Settling into the high-backed leather chair, she picked up the receiver and dialled the overseas code.

She felt a wave of warmth as her mother's voice spoke down the phone. "Lani, sweetheart. How's England. Are you OK? How was your flight? Is the place you're staying in nice?"

"Whoa, rein back there, Mom!" Lani chuckled. "One question at a time."

"Sorry, hon! Your sisters have given me what feels like a small book of things to ask you!"

"How are they?" Lani pictured her three older sisters, Dacil, Guadeloupe and Maria. "Are they all home for Spring Break?"

"Only Dacil," her mother told her. "The others have gone off with friends for the vacation. The house is feeling so empty with your father gone, too! Anyway, tell me all about your trip so far."

Lani filled her in with everything that had happened. "I'll send over loads of photos," she promised. "You won't believe how amazing the house is!"

"I'm so glad you're having a great time," her mother said. "I'm sending you hugs and kisses down the line right now."

"Right back to you," Lani replied before hanging up.

"Good morning!" Amy looked up from her newspaper. "I didn't know what you'd want for breakfast." She waved her hand over the dining room table which was set with eight places. Muffins, bread rolls and miniature packets of cereal were arranged in cloth-lined baskets. "There are scrambled eggs, bacon, sausage and tomato under the covers on the sideboard."

"You guessed all of my favourites," Dylan said appreciatively.

Lani's stomach growled as she headed over to the sideboard to heap egg, sausage and tomato on a plate. It was nearly eleven o'clock British time but Lani's body clock still wasn't totally in sync and it felt much, much earlier.

"I'll give Sally a call if you want your eggs other than scrambled," Amy said

"Poached for me, please," Mrs Harper said as she walked into the room. "Morning, everyone. How did you all sleep?"

"I had this really weird dream that I went home

for Spring Break instead of here and had Morello with me," Dylan said. She paused as she was eating, her fork halfway to her mouth. "I tried putting him in the garage but it was full of boxes, bikes and my dad's car. Then I tried putting him in the backyard and my mum freaked out when he trampled all of her flower beds!"

"I had a strange dream, too." Malory poured herself a glass of juice. "I dreamed that we went back to school but everyone had left and it had been turned into a museum!"

Lani grinned. "It took ages for the *zzzzs* to hit me but when they did I was totally out of it. I was in a no dream zone."

Amy rested her chin on her hands. "I love the way Americans have with language. It's so creative." She smiled fondly at Honey. "When Honey last came to stay everything was cool, totally and major!"

Honey nodded as she bit into her toast. "In school everyone thinks I'm totally English but over here people say how Americanized I am!"

She's still talking as if she's coming back to Chestnut Hill with us, Lani thought wistfully.

The door opened again and Sally walked in followed by Sam and Mr Harper. "Can I get anything for anyone?" Sally asked as she collected up used plates.

"I could really go for a bacon and fried egg roll," Sam said as he sat down next to Honey.

"Good morning," Lani said pointedly.

Sam glanced at her. "Morning," he replied. Lani thought she detected a hint of gloom in his expression before he looked away. *I don't look that bad, do I?*

"I'm glad you're all finally here," Amy said. "I've got some news I've been dying to tell you."

"Dr Starling has called to say she's extending the Spring Break to a month," Lani guessed.

Amy shook her head, her blonde curls bouncing. "Not quite! Meg and I have decided that we'd love to throw a Welcome Home ball. We're going to send out invitations today. We thought we'd hold it on Friday which gives us five days to prepare."

"That sounds wonderful," Mrs Harper enthused. "If it's a warm evening we could have drinks out on the terrace."

Lani swapped an excited look with Malory. *A real British ball in a country house? Talk about the quintessential experience!*

"Meg says she has an entire wardrobe of dresses from her debutante days that you can dive into," Amy told them, "and I believe she's finding a dance instructor to come and give you a few lessons."

"So, will it be a small party?" Dylan's tone was ultra casual as she scooped up a forkful of scrambled eggs.

Lani gave a shout of laughter. "What Dyl means is will there be any eligible bachelors in attendance?"

"I didn't say that." Dylan shot Lani a look of mock outrage.

"No, but you definitely meant it," Honey teased.

Dylan took a breath to respond and then exhaled. "Yeah." She grinned. "Bang to rights, I did mean that."

"I'm sure we'll be able to rustle up a few unattached

young men." Amy sounded amused. "And I'm sure the Harper men will put on a good show."

Mr Harper winked at Sam. "Not if I'm expected to wear a suit."

Mrs Harper raised her eyes heavenward and then turned to Honey. "What are your plans today, sweetheart?"

"No, hang on," Sam interrupted. He pressed his fingers against his temples and closed his eyes. "I have something coming through. . . I think . . . I'm fairly sure I can see stable doors, muck heaps, horses. . ."

"I'm not convinced that knowing the girls will be zooming over to Home Farm makes you psychic," Mr Harper commented as he pushed back his chair. "Your mum and I are off to trail estate agents' windows this morning to draw up a property shortlist. Do you want to come?"

"Um, it's a tough one but I think I'll hang out with the girls," Sam replied.

Lani's heart skipped a beat. *Maybe now Sam will thaw out and tell me exactly what's been bugging him since we started this trip.*

"Why are your parents looking for somewhere to rent? Couldn't they just stay here?" Dylan asked as they headed out to the old stables adjacent to the house. Lani counted eight looseboxes, all of which had their doors bolted shut.

"I think Dad wants to be closer to the university," Honey explained.

"And, while staying here is great, Mum and Dad like their own space," Sam added.

"Do your aunt and uncle ride?" Malory asked as they drew near the red-brick stable block.

"No." Honey shook her head. "I think the last time these stables had any proper use was when Meg was much younger." She tugged back the bolt on the end loosebox. "Most of them are used for storage now, although Uncle Timothy converted one into a gym." Pulling back the door, she revealed a spacious loosebox filled with gardening tools, ladders and a row of bikes in a stand.

Honey pointed at the blue mountain bike at the end of the stand. "Lani, you'd better take Dad's since you've got the longest legs."

Sam stepped forward and Lani thought he was getting the bike out for her. When she saw him grasp the handles of a metallic green bike halfway along the rack, the thanks died on her lips. Not that she needed his help, but it would have been a nice gesture. Trying to push down her annoyance, Lani took hold of her bike's handlebars. She wheeled it into the yard and looked around for Sam. She turned at the sound of crunching gravel. Sam was riding slowly around the walled pond in front of the main house. *Relax*, Lani told herself. *Now's not the time. Sort it out with him later*. Yesterday she'd been upset at the way Sam was blanking her. Now she was accelerating towards plain mad. She swung her leg over the saddle and waited for the others to bring their bikes out.

"OK." Honey pushed out her bike. "Is everyone ready?"

"How far away is Home Farm?" Malory asked, following Honey out of the stable.

"Across country it's less than a mile but around the lanes it's more like three," Honey replied. Setting her foot on the pedal, she pushed off. From the corner of her eye, Lani watched Sam complete a final circuit of the pond before putting on a spurt of speed to catch up.

Honey led them down the gently curving drive. Lani cycled just behind her, admiring the towering avenue of trees. It wasn't too hard to imagine the days when horse-drawn carriages would sweep up the driveway, carrying lords and ladies in their evening finery. As they approached the gated entrance, Honey put on her brakes. They squealed as if the bike hadn't been used in a while, and Honey glanced back at Lani, pulling a face. Dismounting, she pushed her bike over to a small side gate set further down in the wall. Once everyone was through, Honey turned right and began to pedal down the lane.

As Lani rode along she wished the hedgerows were lower so she could see into the fields on the other side. She felt as if she'd cycled into a picture book! Heady scents filled the air and bumble bees hovered over white flowers growing in the hedge.

Honey turned off the main road, down a single track lane. The hedgerows were lower here and Lani's bike wobbled as she gazed at the surrounding countryside.

Very clean-looking black and white cows strolled in the meadows, and in one field half a dozen lambs were taking turns to jump on and off a tree stump.

Dylan looked over her shoulder as Lani's front tyre bumped against her back one. "I've just discovered something worse than you overcrowding me on Colorado, and it's you overcrowding me on a bike!"

"Yikes, sorry," Lani said, squeezing her brake handle. She dropped back and steered closer to the edge of the lane, until the heavy white flower heads brushed against her knee. On either side of the lane, rolling farmland had given way to tidy green pastures divided by white post-and-rail fencing. Lani strained to see any sign of horses but had to snap her attention back to the road as Honey turned right. After a few hundred metres the lane curved around to the left and to her delight Lani spotted half a dozen horses grazing. Alongside three of the mares were leggy chestnut newborns. One of them nuzzled its mother's flank, its short tail whisking frantically as it tried to find the milk.

"Oh my gosh!" she shrieked. "Foals!"

"They're the older mares," Honey called back. "Henry's breeding stock."

Lani ran her eyes over the Thoroughbreds' sleek lines and intelligent-shaped heads. She felt a skip of excitement. They were gorgeous!

"How many horses are there on the yard?" Malory asked.

"About thirty, but it changes," Honey shouted over her shoulder. "Henry buys and sells all the time."

They rode up to a five-bar gate which had the words *Dysart Home Farm* printed on a nameplate. Sam shot past in a spurt of speed and braked with a dramatic flourish. He half skidded to a halt and jumped off. Unhooking the clasp, he pushed open the gate.

Lani got off her bike and wheeled it along a short stretch of track which led to the main yard. In front of her was a long row of stables with a sloping tiled roof. On each side of the main row were two shorter runs of stables framing the yard. Horses looked over some of the doors, their ears pricked with curiosity.

With a sudden eruption of barking two Border Terriers came running out of an empty stable. "Merlin, Poppy!" A middle-aged man whose dark hair was peppered with grey strode after the dogs. When he saw Honey and Sam, his face broke into a smile. "Hi, you two. Meg said you were back home."

"Hi, Henry," Honey greeted him.

Henry ran his gaze over Lani, Malory and Dylan. "I hear you're over from the States. How are you enjoying things so far?"

"We keep thinking things can't get any better and yet somehow they do," Lani responded. She felt a bit like a racehorse being judged under Henry's cool blue eyes.

"Glad to hear it," Henry said. He glanced at his watch. "I'm due up on the Downs to watch one of our two-year-olds run. Clancy's around if you need anything." He whistled to the dogs. "I'll see you later."

"Up on the Downs?" Dylan frowned. "Is it me or does that make no sense?"

"The name Downs comes from the old English term 'dun'. It means hill," Sam explained as he pushed his bike into a stand.

Lani put her bike alongside Sam's before going over to make friends with a handsome bay Thoroughbred. "Pop Idol." She read the name plate on the stable door. "Hi there, boy." She reached out and gently ran her hand down the gelding's nose.

"Careful, or he'll have you doing that all day," a cheerful voice called in a broad Irish accent.

"Hey, Clancy." Lani turned to see Sam putting up his hand to give a short, narrow-hipped young man a high five.

"Clancy's the head lad," Honey said as she secured her bike. "As opposed to the travelling head lad, which is a different job. Clancy, these are my friends, Lani, Dylan and Malory."

"Glad to meet you." Clancy's bright blue eyes danced as he flashed them a smile. "I see you're already making friends." He nodded at Pop Idol.

"He's lovely," Lani admitted.

In the next stable down a grey looked out over the door and gave a soft whicker. "Hey, Hazel," Clancy said. "You're wondering if you're missing out on any action, huh?"

Dylan and Malory both headed over to make a fuss of her. "Great minds think alike," Dylan said with a grin.

"So how's everything going?" Honey asked Clancy. "Has Henry had many winners lately?"

Clancy hesitated. "To tell the truth, we've hit a run of

bad luck." He took off his cap and ran his hand through his dark hair. "Our best runner slipped on the gallops two weeks ago and is out of action."

"Not Zhivago's Colonel?" Honey gasped.

Clancy nodded. "By the time he's recovered and his fitness has been brought back up, he'll have missed the Newmarket races. Our second best horse, I Should Be So Lucky, has been losing form and had to be pulled up in his last race. We've just had the results back from his blood tests and he's anaemic."

An elderly man dressed in breeches and an ancient-looking jacket stepped out of a nearby stall. He began cleaning a body brush with a curry comb while tilting his head in Clancy's direction to listen to the conversation.

"We're laying everything on Dardanus now," Clancy told them. "He's running in the Classic Cup a week Wednesday."

"Dardanus belongs to Meg," Honey explained. "He's by Golden Age out of Cleopatra, who are both Group One winners. Cleopatra is the dam of two stake winners including the 2006 Breeders' Cup Turf." Her voice held a note of pride.

Malory looked around the yard. "Where is he?"

"Up on the gallops," Clancy replied. "I need to get the afternoon feeds ready now, but if you want anything give me a shout."

There was a clatter of hooves as two Thoroughbreds were led out on to the yard. Their two riders used the mounting block to get on the horses before checking their girths. As the rider on the bay tightened her girth, her horse's ears flashed back. Baring his teeth, the bay snapped at the chestnut alongside him.

"Whoa!" the chestnut's rider shouted as his horse skittered sideways. He shortened his reins and kicked the chestnut forward, away from the bay horse's snaking neck.

The elderly man shook his head as he finished cleaning the body brush. "I'm surprised that wasn't a lot worse," he muttered, chewing on the piece of straw sticking out of his mouth.

"Why's that, Reg?" Sam asked.

"The curse," Reg said ominously. He leaned against Pop Idol's door. The bay snuffled Reg's shoulder. The old man reached up and stroked the gelding's nose.

Malory's eyes widened. "What curse?"

"The curse of Dysart Hall," Reg told them. He looked at each of them, and Lani got the feeling he was enjoying the drama. "The inheritance of Dysart is supposed to be passed directly down the Dysart line. Now that line has been broken, the curse has been triggered."

Sam frowned. "The line hasn't been broken. Meg's husband was a direct descendant of the first Lord Dysart, and Dysart Hall's been passed to their son, Uncle Timothy."

"Yes, but who's running Dysart Farm?" Reg raised his white eyebrows. "Henry Stilling, that's who. And who had approached Lord Timothy with an offer to buy Dysart Farm just before all of our luck began to run bad? Henry Stilling again. He's only a cousin, which means he's not part of the direct line. That's where the root of all our troubles lies."

Honey shook her head. "You don't really believe in curses, do you, Reg?"

"I believe in this curse," Reg insisted. "I've seen the evidence of it with my own eyes these past few weeks. I'm telling you, old Lord Dysart's ghost is angry and until Henry drops this idea of buying Home Farm, things will only get worse."

Lani felt a shiver run up her spine. Even though she didn't believe in ghosts, there was something unnerving about the intensity in Reg's eyes.

Dylan gave a low whistle. "Well, I guess no English ancestral pile would be complete without an ancestral ghost."

Reg took the straw out of his mouth and pointed it at Dylan. "You may choose to make light of it, young lady, but I'm telling you, there's worse to come. You mark my words. We've yet to feel the full force of old Lord Dysart's fury."

"This place is absolutely amazing," Lani gasped as Honey showed them another run of stables backing on to the main row.

"That's the dormitory where the stable lads and lasses sleep." Honey pointed to two single storey buildings. "And that's the Rec." She nodded at the adjacent barn.

Malory raised an eyebrow. "Rec?"

"Recreation," Sam answered her. "It's where they eat and hang out in their free time." He headed towards the large glass door halfway along the side of the barn. "I'll catch up with you guys later."

Honey smiled. "Sam has an ongoing pool tournament with some of the lads. It may only take place a couple of times a year but that doesn't mean they forget about it!"

A young woman with a helmet tucked under her arm headed out of a second, smaller barn. She waved. "Hi, Honey!"

"Jess!" Honey hurried over and hugged her. "It's

really good to see you again!" She turned to the others, "Jess is the travelling head lad, as I was saying earlier."

"I'm guessing you're Lani, Dylan and Malory." Jess smiled at the three girls. "Honey talked about you all the time during her last visit."

"Guilty as charged," Dylan admitted.

"Clancy asked if you want to ride out?" Jess shook back her curly strawberry-blonde hair before tucking the curls into her riding helmet and buckling the chin strap. "I'm about to take a string out for some road work. I'm sure their riders would swap that for an extended lunch break." She grinned at the girls. "We won't go any faster than a trot, but you'll get a good idea of what it feels like to be a jockey on one of our long-legged beasties!"

Lani's heart flipped with excitement. *I'm going to ride a real racehorse!*

"They're already tacked up," Jess added. "You'll be riding Woody, Sara, Rousty and Romeo. Grab some hats from the tack room."

The tack room was inside the barn and reminded Lani of the one at Chestnut Hill. Row upon row of polished leather saddles and bridles lined the walls. *Except they're a lot smaller than the ones we use*, Lani thought as she ran her hand over a lightweight racing saddle. It felt like little more than a saddle pad, with slender string girths and papery stirrup leathers. It couldn't have been more different from the heavy wooden-framed Western saddles that she had learned to ride on. She took a spare hat and followed Honey on to the main yard.

Honey pointed at the opposite row of stables. "We're riding the older horses," she said. "They're not as lively as the younger ones!"

Lani pulled back the bolt of one of the stables Honey had pointed out. She read the nameplate. "Sandalwood."

"His yard name's Woody," Honey called. Lani figured it made sense that each racehorse would have a shorter pet name; their official names could be quite a mouthful!

Inside a bright chestnut gelding blew through his nostrils at her. Lani tipped back her head and stared up at the horse's long, intelligent face. *Colorado could walk under Woody's stomach and still have some clearance!* "Where's the stepladder?" she joked as she reached out to take hold of Woody. She released his reins from where they'd been looped through the throat lash and then led him out on to the yard. Her stomach churned with a mixture of nerves and excitement as she walked Woody over to the mounting block. "Come on, cowgirl," she murmured, using her family's nickname for her. "You wanted to see what was over those hedgerows and now you're going to get your chance." She swung her leg over the saddle and squeezed Woody away from the block so the others could mount.

As they rode off the yard, following Jess's lead, Lani was surprised by how quickly she adjusted to Woody's height. His stride was long and fluid and he carried his head high. She ran her hand down his neck. *This is so cool! My first proper day in England and already I'm riding!* It felt strange riding with such short stirrups and Lani didn't feel too secure as she tried to relax in the saddle. *I'm glad it's just road work we're doing*, she thought as they broke into a trot, although part of her loved the idea of riding Woody at a flat out gallop.

"Is this amazing or what?" Dylan called from behind her. Lani glanced over her shoulder. Dylan was riding Romeo, a dark bay gelding with a dramatic broad blaze.

"Amazing," Lani agreed.

They walked and trotted for what felt like miles and Lani was amazed at how far the Dysart estate stretched; every time she called to Honey to ask if this was still Meg's land, Honey nodded. *I can understand anyone fighting to keep Dysart in the family, but a ghost? I don't think so!* A shaft of sunlight burst from behind a cloud and Lani suddenly felt foolish for letting Reg's words get to her even one teeny bit. Up ahead, Malory moved easily to a dark chestnut gelding's stride. She looked as if she had been riding racehorses for years. Lani smiled, admiring her friend's natural talent.

From the front of the file, Jess called, "Look to your right!" A hill towered above them but Lani's attention was grabbed by the giant white horse carved into it. Long sweeping lines of chalk sketched out a racehorse in full gallop over the smooth green land.

"It's thousands of years old," Honey announced.

So it can't be a racehorse! The sport hasn't been around that long! Lani shook her head in amazement. Who had carved those lines into the turf? It seemed amazing that people had loved horses for their beauty and speed so long ago.

Lani's attention snapped back to Woody as he threw up his head and broke out of his steady pace. Lani couldn't resist allowing him to canter a few strides before she brought him back to a trot. She was beginning to feel a lot more secure in the saddle, and had figured out how to grip with her knees rather than the full length of her leg. She'd love to allow Woody to open up and show what he had! "It's just walking and trotting today," she told Woody as she brought him back under control. The chestnut tossed his head and danced on the spot, feeling like a tightly coiled spring. Lani glanced at the rolling countryside and hoped that they would get to gallop before going home.

That would be the icing on the English cake!

Meg held up one of the dresses she had laid out in her private sitting room for the girls to try. "This is a Pierre Balmain," she said, a note of wistfulness in her voice. "I wore it at my first hunt ball." The dark blue silk dress was embroidered with shimmering bugle beads and silver sequins. She held it out to Malory. "It would suit your colouring perfectly."

Dylan held a green silk evening dress against herself. Its crystal-encrusted bodice glittered against the light. "This is amazing."

"It's Pucci." Meg smiled. "One of Marilyn Monroe's favourite designers. In fact, she was buried in her green silk Pucci dress."

"Which one are you wearing?" Lani asked Honey.

Honey hesitated. "I've already got a dress," she

admitted. "I bought it the last time I was here when Aunt Amy threw a summer barbeque and dance. Mum's going to give me a stole but apart from that I'm all set."

Lani looked at the dresses that were left. They were all meringue affairs with huge frothy petticoats. She felt a stab of disappointment. None of them would look good on her. While she prided herself on being a tomboy and rarely wore a dress, when it came to a party she didn't want to feel a total reject.

Meg had obviously reached the same conclusion. Shaking her head, she pronounced, "None of these will do!" She narrowed her eyes as she looked Lani up and down. "You're a British size eight, am I right?"

Lani did a quick sum in her head and nodded.

A smile played on Meg's lips. "Leave it to me." Waving her hands, she sent Dylan and Malory out of the room to find the dressmaker who was waiting for them in the library. "Now," Meg said, "while they're being measured so their dresses can be adjusted, we'll start thinking about the dancing!"

Lani felt her stomach twisting with nerves. Dancing wasn't exactly her strong suit. "How much will we be expected to know?"

"Oh, the burden for getting the steps right will be on the men," Meg said cheerfully. "You'll be following their lead, after all! I've booked the dance instructor to come every afternoon between now and the ball so I'm sure you'll be fine."

Lani doubted it but she didn't want to hurt Meg's feelings so she tried to make herself look positive.

Moments later the dance instructor, a slender woman in her fifties wearing a long floral coat and a bright turquoise turban, walked in with Amy.

"Good morning," said the dance instructor with a warm smile. "My name is Melissa. I understand we have a ballroom emergency?"

Meg nodded. "Welcome, Melissa, thank you so much for coming. These young ladies need to be able to dance with their heads held high by Friday evening, if possible."

Melissa didn't look daunted by the task, although Lani figured she might change her mind once she saw their current standard of dancing. "Do we have any gallant dancing partners?" Melissa asked.

"I've roped in some volunteers," Amy said cheerfully. She waved her hand behind her. Tom looked around the door and waggled his eyebrows theatrically before stepping into the room. He was followed by two of the gardeners and, after a pause, Sam. Lani's heart began to pound as she realized that now Sam would have to acknowledge her.

The dance instructor walked over to the grand piano in the corner of the room and experimented with a few notes. "All right," she said. "Let's try a few basic moves." She nodded at Meg. "Can you demonstrate for us, Meg?"

Meg stepped on to the floor and held out her arms. "There was a day when I'd have had young men fighting to be the one to have the privilege to dance with me."

Tom walked towards her. "And now we all realize

that none of us can hold a candle to you," he told her. Meg's eyes twinkled. The music began and together they waltzed around the floor.

Melissa provided a commentary. "The basic ballroom waltz steps are made up of three movements. The man steps forward, putting his right leg between his partner's legs, then he takes his left leg forward and to the side, then he closes right to left. In the next bar he steps backward on his left, and it's the lady's turn to step forward on the right."

Lani gulped. That sounded more like instructions for falling in a heap.

Dylan and Malory walked back through the double doors. "I could never dance like that," Dylan sighed.

"You read my thoughts," Lani said without taking her eyes off Meg and Tom.

The music came to an end and Melissa glanced at the girls. "If you would partner up, we'll begin."

Lani glanced expectantly at Sam. He hesitated and then walked over to Honey with his hands held out. Honey looked flustered. Swallowing hard, and trying to look as if she didn't care, Lani walked over to one of the gardeners. He grinned nervously at her as they took each other's hands – not the formal ballroom hold, but a beginner's hold, Melissa explained. As they began to shuffle around to the music, Lani couldn't bring herself to care if she messed up the steps or not. All she could think about was the way that Sam had deliberately snubbed her.

I guess this means he's breaking up with me, she

thought miserably. *And he doesn't even have the guts to tell me to my face.*

Lani pushed her vegetables around the plate, wondering if she'd ever feel like eating again. *Is this it? Is Sam going to carry on ignoring me until I go home?* She felt a surge of anger. She thought what they'd had was special. How could he act like nothing had ever happened between them?

"Did you find anything you liked?" Amy asked Honey's parents who had got back from their house-hunting just in time for dinner.

"We've narrowed it down to two properties," Mrs Harper responded. "They're both in the same village just twenty minutes away from Oxford and half an hour's drive from Honey and Sam's school." She smiled at Honey. "You'll be glad to know that there's a local riding school on the edge of the village."

Honey gave a small tight smile and Lani read her mind as clearly as if the words had appeared in a speech bubble over Honey's head. *What does it matter that there's a riding school nearby when Minnie's in a different country?* Lani's stomach twisted at the reminder that soon five thousand miles would be separating her from the twins.

"What are the houses like?" Sam asked.

"One's a converted barn," Mrs Harper said. "It's really airy with rafters and wooden floors throughout but it's got a tiny garden."

"And the other?" Sam prompted.

"The other one is a cottage," Mr Harper told him. "It's got four bedrooms, one of which would make a great shared study."

"And it's got a huge garden," Mrs Harper said enthusiastically, "which backs on to woodland."

"They both sound nice." Honey picked up the gravy boat and poured it over her beef. "When can we have a look at them?"

"We've arranged a viewing first thing in the morning," Mr Harper said. "We'll have to make up our minds soon before somebody else snaps them up."

Honey glanced down and bit her lip. Lani knew how tough it was going to be for her to face the reality that she wasn't coming back to Chestnut Hill. *But Sam,* she thought bitterly, *is acting as if his time in the States meant nothing. How can he act like he can't wait to move back to the UK? Isn't there anything he's disappointed to be leaving behind?*

Honey was quiet as they headed over to the yard the next afternoon. Lani was dying to ask how the house viewing had gone but she sensed that her friend didn't want to talk about it. Sam had been dropped off in Oxford to meet up with friends and while part of Lani was disappointed, another part was relieved. *I need some time out to prepare for the showdown that's got to happen,* she acknowledged. She was determined to confront Sam about the way he was treating her. But she needed to do it when they had their own private space.

As Home Farm came into sight, Lani asked Honey, "Are you OK?"

Honey sighed. "Everything's suddenly so. . ." She hesitated. ". . .permanent."

Lani reached over and squeezed her arm. Before she could say anything there was a volley of barking and a startled shout. Swapping bemused glances, the girls pushed their bikes on to the yard to see Merlin and Poppy being chased by two miniature versions of themselves. Jess and another stable lad were trying to catch the puppies who neatly evaded their every dive.

"Merlin, Poppy, come!" Honey whistled and the two dogs bounded over to greet her with the puppies in fast pursuit. As Honey made a fuss of the older dogs she gestured to her friends to capture the puppies who were trying to grasp hold of their parents' wagging tails. Dylan and Malory caught one, while Lani scooped up the other, laughing as the puppy licked her chin with its tiny pink tongue.

"Thanks, guys," Jess said breathlessly. "I can't believe we didn't think of catching Poppy and Merlin instead of going for the puppies."

Malory gently stroked her puppy's head. "They're so cute."

"They're a couple of escape artists!" Jess groaned. "The rest of the litter have gone to new homes but nobody's taken these two." She pushed her hair off her forehead. "Henry insists on the yard always being immaculate because we never know when an owner is going to turn up. Having two puppies running around the place isn't the best advert for professionalism!"

"What are their names?" Dylan giggled as the puppy she was holding tried to chew her hair.

"You've got Peanut and Lani's holding Chip," Jess told her. "They're supposed to be kept in the top loosebox." She pointed across the yard. "If they're ever not there then you'll find them terrorizing Merlin and Poppy or scheming to get into the chicken pen alongside Henry's house."

"We'll keep that in mind," Lani said as Chip struggled to get down. "Do you want us to put them away now?"

"Please," Jess said. "We're running really late."

"We're here to help," Honey told her. "What do you need a hand with?"

"If you could fetch tack for Dardanus, Early Dawn, Major Difference and Starlight Express, that would be great," Jess said. "Once they've been taken up to the gallops, their mangers and buckets need scrubbing out. They all just lift out of their brackets. Don't get them mixed up with the other buckets about the place. All drinking buckets are black, and we use yellow buckets for washing."

"We're on it." Lani pulled a salute, touching her fingers to her dark hair.

They collected the sets of tack and carried them back to the main yard. Lani had Dardanus' tack and headed down to the grey's stall. "Hi," she said to the stable lad who was grooming the gelding. "Jess asked me to bring these." She placed the tack on the door.

The stable lad looked up. A puzzled look passed over his face.

"I'm Lani. I'm staying with Honey for the week," Lani told him.

The boy's expression cleared. "I thought you were a bit young to be an apprentice! I'm Wayne."

"Are you an apprentice?" Lani asked curiously.

"I sure am," Wayne said cheerfully.

"What does that involve?" Lani brushed her arm over a speck of dust on the seat of the saddle.

"Well, at the moment most of my work is caring for the horses," Wayne told her. "I'm in charge of three and ride them out each day. I'm being trained up by Clancy and Henry so I can reach the point where I can apply for a licence to race."

"Is it tough?" Lani asked.

Wayne laughed. "The toughest thing is keeping my weight in between eight and nine stone." He looked rail thin to Lani, and his shoulder blades jutted out beneath the fabric of his T-shirt; she felt a stab of sympathy for him, especially if he enjoyed food as much as she did.

"Jess mentioned something about owners," Lani said. "But I thought that Lord Timothy owned the yard?"

Wayne scraped the body brush over the curry comb. "Jess was talking about the racehorse owners."

Lani's fingers itched to be able to groom Dardanus. The gelding half closed his eyes as Wayne worked the body brush in smooth strokes over his pale stone-coloured coat. "How many owners are there?"

67

"Lots!" Wayne told her with a grin. "Most of the horses here are owned by more than one person. Present company excluded." He patted the gelding's shoulder. "You're Meg's pride and joy, aren't you, Dandy?"

Lani smiled. She was glad she wasn't the only one to speak to horses as if she expected them to answer her back!

"Henry's always on the look out for new owners to move their horses to the yard," Wayne continued. "It's why the yard always has to look its best in case prospective owners visit. It's also why Henry's runners need to make a good showing whenever they race. Henry's livelihood depends on his reputation."

Lani nodded. She hadn't realized how precarious running a racing yard could be, but it made sense when Wayne put it like that.

Wayne held out a comb. "Do you want to do his mane and tail?"

"You bet!" Lani pulled back the bolt and stepped into the loosebox. Dardanus shifted restlessly. "Easy, lad," Lani murmured. She held out her hand for Dardanus to sniff. The gelding's ears swivelled forwards and he blew through his nostrils. "There's a good boy," Lani said as she drew the comb through the silky grey mane.

Wayne glanced at his watch. "Time to tack up." He shot Lani a mischievous glance. "I don't suppose you'd like to ride Dandy out for me, too?"

Lani's eyes widened before she realized she was being teased. "Hey! You got me there for a moment!"

"And there was I thinking Americans didn't get the

Brits' sense of humour." Wayne grinned as he lifted the tiny saddle on to the grey's back.

"Hey, just because our sense of humour is way more sophisticated, doesn't mean we don't recognize your attempts at it," Lani shot back.

"Fair play!" Wayne laughed as he buckled on his helmet. "Thanks for your help, Lani. I'll see you around."

Lani stood back for him to lead the racehorse out of the stall. "Now that," she called after Wayne, "I can guarantee!"

Lani's eyes flew open and she stared unseeingly into the dark. "You guys!" she whispered. "Did any of you just hear something?"

"I did," Malory whispered back from the other side of the four-poster bed. From the even sound of breathing in the room it was obvious that Honey and Dylan had slept through the loud clanging noise.

"I think it came from over by the window. What do you think it was?" Lani hissed.

"I don't know." Malory suddenly spoke in a normal voice. "Why are we whispering?"

"What's going on?" Honey sounded sleepy. There was the sound of fumbling and then light flooded the room.

Before Lani could reply, there was a creak followed by a thud.

"What was that?" Honey sat up, looking startled. She reached across and prodded Dylan. "Dyl, wake up! How can you sleep through this?"

Dylan blinked. "What time is it?"

Lani glanced at the clock on the mantelpiece. "It's 5.15."

"In the *morning?*" Dylan sounded scandalized.

"Well, it's not going to be in the afterno. . ." Lani broke off as another clank rang out. "I'm sure that came from up above us. Hon, what's above us?"

"The attics." Honey hugged her knees against her chest. "But no one ever goes up there."

"You know what this is." Dylan raked her hand through her red hair. "This is the ghost of Lord Dysart."

Malory gasped and dove under the duvet. "I don't believe in ghosts," she said with a muffled yelp.

"Oh, really? Because you're sure giving a convincing performance of someone who does," Dylan pointed out.

"This is ridiculous," Lani muttered, pushing back her bedcovers. "Come on. We're going on a ghost hunt."

"You're crazy!" Dylan exclaimed. "I'm not going anywhere."

"Well, I am." Lani sounded braver than she felt. Grabbing up her dressing gown, she tied the belt around her waist and headed to the door.

"Hang on!" Honey called. "We can't let you go on your own!"

Feeling a rush of relief, Lani waited for her friends to join her. "Shouldn't we have a torch?" Malory's voice was low as Dylan opened the door.

"Oh, hang on. I left it on my bedstand, beside the coil of rope and bucket of sand in case of other emergencies." Dylan's voice was loaded with irony.

"FYI, there are people out there who keep torches in their bedrooms," Malory told her.

Dylan's response was cut off by another loud clank.

Lani crept into the darkened hallway. "How do we get up into the attics?" she asked Honey.

"Guys, this is insane," Malory whispered as Honey pointed down the landing.

They crept, single file, to the staircase. Lani stopped at the bottom and Honey bumped into her. "Sorry," Honey hissed. "There's a door at the top which leads into the attics."

Lani could just make out the dark form of the staircase with a narrow chink of light at the top. She grasped the twisted rope that acted as a handgrip and began to make her way up the stairs. With each loud creak from the treads, Lani's heart rate accelerated. She half hoped the door would be locked as she brushed her hand over its handle. She bit her lip as the door swung open.

Early morning light spilled into the room from the uncovered windows. Lani looked about, seeing nothing but dustsheets covering different-shaped objects and stacks of packing cases.

Suddenly Dylan gave a loud shriek. Lani spun around and gazed in the direction Dylan was pointing. A dusty suit of armour loomed in the corner of the attic. Before anyone could speak another clang sounded right from where the armour stood.

"It's Lord Dysart!" Dylan gasped.

"I'm out of here!" Malory turned and raced for the door.

Lani's nerve finally broke and she bolted after the others. They pounded down the stairs and as they raced down the landing one of the bedroom doors opened.

"What's going on?" Amy looked out, her blonde hair tousled. Her eyes were bleary as she blinked at the girls.

"Lord Dysart's armour!" Dylan panted. "It's coming alive!"

Amy raised her eyebrows sceptically. "You mean the Victorian fake armour that was made, oh, at least four hundred years after Lord Dysart was alive?"

"But we heard noises," Malory told her.

"The central heating makes a dreadful racket in Meg's old room," Amy explained. "That's what all that clanging would have been. Sorry, I should have warned you."

Lani turned and gave Dylan's arm a shove. "Lord Dysart's ghost!"

"Suit of armour coming to life!" Honey's lips trembled with laughter.

Dylan planted her hands on her hips. "OK, so there's an explanation this time, but that doesn't mean there isn't a ghost." As they turned to head back to their room she muttered, "And I swear I saw that armour move."

Lani tugged up the zip on her waterproof jacket. "One thing you're sure not winning with your country swap is the climate."

Honey grimaced at the rain which was coming down in a fine drizzle. "There are lots of things I'm not winning," she said quietly.

The girls stored their bikes and walked on to the yard. Jess was washing down the concrete surface with a hose while one of the stable lads swept after her. From Peanut's and Chip's stall came yelping and whining.

"Do you think we should go and see them?" Malory suggested.

Honey nodded. "They probably want some company."

The girls headed over to the puppies' stall and Honey pulled back the bolt. The second she started to open the door, the puppies squeezed through the tiny gap. "Grab them!" Honey cried.

Lani grasped Peanut's scruff but the puppy wriggled free. With a groan, Lani watched Peanut chase down the yard after Chip.

"Get those dogs back in their stall!" Henry looked out of Pop Idol's stall. He frowned at the puppies and then at the girls. "Now! Before they cause even more trouble!"

Lani swapped an alarmed glance with Malory. *Talk about an overreaction.* They hurried down the yard and caught the puppies who had crouched low to the ground with their tails clamped between their legs when Henry started shouting.

"Come on," Lani crooned to Peanut. "Let's get you back to your playroom." The girls carried Peanut and Chip back into the stall and gave them their favourite toys – a short piece of rope for tug-of-war, and a squeaky plastic bone. Once the puppies were scampering happily around the sawdust floor, the girls slipped out.

Jess hurried up to make sure both bolts were in place.

"What's wrong with Henry?" Honey asked in a low voice. "He seems super-tense."

"We've got a really important prospective owner visiting this morning," Jess explained. "His name's Daniel Blanchett and he owns a string of six Group One horses. He's looking for a new training yard and it will be a real coup if he decides to put his horses with us."

"The windows in the lower stalls haven't been cleaned." Clancy strode across the yard towards them. "Who was supposed to be doing them?"

"I'll get them sorted now," Jess said quickly.

Clancy nodded as he walked into one of the top boxes.

Jess puffed at a strand of hair that had fallen over her cheek. "Sarah, one of the lasses, was supposed to do them last night but she was called away. Her mother's been taken into hospital with suspected appendicitis."

"We'll take care of the windows," Malory volunteered.

Jess looked grateful. "That would be great. I've had to share Sarah's work out so everyone's already juggling more than usual."

The girls headed down to the tack room and each took a yellow bucket. They filled them with hot soapy water and carried them over to the empty run of looseboxes opposite.

As Lani carefully rubbed her cloth over the windowpane, she heard someone walk into the loosebox. Turning, she saw Clancy. "The bedding's not deep enough in the corners." He clicked his tongue with annoyance. "We don't want Blanchett thinking we're amateurs."

"I'll fetch more shavings as soon as I finish the window," Lani offered.

Clancy nodded before turning on his heel and walking away. Lani stared after him, surprised by how uptight he was. *This is such a big deal for everyone.*

As soon as she was done cleaning the window she put away her bucket and went to find another pack of shavings.

Wayne passed her carrying a striped blanket. "Nothing like a bit of organized chaos!" He winked.

"Lucky you if you're organized," another stable lad groaned. He rattled his grooming box. "I've still got to groom Star."

"I'll give you a hand," Wayne said easily. "Can't have you letting Team Stilling down, can I?"

Lani lugged the plastic bag of shavings over to the loosebox. Deftly she split the plastic and shook out the lemon-scented sawdust. She heaped it into the corners of the box and stood back to make sure her efforts would pass inspection.

"Lani!" Dylan stood in the entrance and flapped her hands. "He's here!"

Lani picked up the torn plastic before hurrying after Dylan to peep around the stable block. Honey and Malory made room for them.

"He looks like a Mafioso!" Dylan whispered.

Lani grinned. Daniel Blanchett had just stepped out of a dark blue BMW. He wore oversized dark sunglasses and a perfectly tailored black suit. His driver came around to hold an umbrella over him. Daniel Blanchett took it and gestured for the driver to get back in the car.

"Mr Blanchett, welcome." Henry shook hands with the visitor. He gestured to the first loosebox to begin the tour of the yard. From inside Wayne reached over the loosebox door to open it for the two men.

Suddenly Honey gasped. "The puppies' loosebox! It's open!"

"It can't be. We bolted it and Jess double-checked." Lani looked over Honey's shoulder. Her eyes widened as she saw that the door was ajar. "One of us will have to go and lock it."

"What happens if the puppies are already out?" Malory whispered.

"We spread out and find them, quickly." Honey sounded grim. "We can't let them do anything to spoil this new client's visit."

"*Prospective* new client," Lani couldn't help pointing out. *And it's unlikely to go further than that if two puppies start clambering up his bespoke suit.*

"I'll go," Dylan volunteered.

"Wait until they're inside the next loosebox," Lani said as Henry and Daniel Blanchett came out from seeing Dardanus.

Henry had his hand on the stable door when there was a sudden racket.

"Oh no," Lani whispered.

Peanut raced across the yard with Chip in pursuit. In Peanut's mouth was a flapping bundle of brown and red feathers.

Malory's hand flew up to her mouth. "He's got one of the chickens!"

Chip's excited yapping was nearly drowned by the chicken's terrified squawks. Several of the horses whinnied in fright and backed into their boxes.

Daniel Blanchett's brows furrowed as he stared at the puppies.

Taking a quick breath, Lani dashed out on to the yard. She made a grab for Peanut and held him down. "Drop!"

Peanut let go of the uninjured but startled chicken. Lani gently scooped it up and tucked it under her arm. Feathers floated down, one of them landing on Peanut's head like a soft little hat. Lani might have found the situation amusing if so much hadn't been resting on this visit going smoothly. Dylan and Malory hurried up to shoo the puppies into their box and lock it.

Honey exchanged a worried look with Lani. "I'll show you where the chicken run is."

Lani followed Honey the short distance down to the farmhouse. A woman with her hair held back by a headscarf was standing at the garden gate. Lani guessed she was Henry's wife. "I saw what happened out of the kitchen window." She took the chicken from Lani and checked it over. "I don't understand how the puppies got into the chicken run. It's totally secure." Her face looked strained. "Of all the days for something like this to happen."

"I'm really sorry, Becky." Honey squeezed the woman's arm. "The puppies are locked away now."

"Just like they were before," Lani muttered as they left Becky. "How did they get out?"

As soon as Henry took Daniel Blanchett down on to the second yard, the girls broke into conversation.

"Somebody opened the puppies' stall," Malory said.

"Or something," Dylan said ominously.

"Oh, come on, Dyl! You're not saying that it was Lord Dysart's ghost who pulled back the bolts on the door and then opened the chicken run?" Lani knew that Dylan had a wild imagination but this was too much for anyone to believe.

Dylan shrugged. "Why would anyone else want to wreck Daniel Blanchett's visit?"

"Oh no," Honey groaned. "Look." She pointed at one of the top stalls. A dark pool of liquid seeped from underneath the door.

Honey looked over her shoulders. "Quick, let's sort it out before they come back up."

They rushed over to the stall and pulled back the door. Inside a grey mare blinked at them in surprise. Lani glanced down at the bucket holders and her eyes widened as she saw that the water container was upended on the floor.

"How did that come out of its holder?" Malory asked.

"We'll worry about that later," Dylan said darkly. "For now let's just worry about getting this mess cleaned up."

Lani picked up the bucket to get a refill while Honey hurried to fetch a broom. As she held the bucket under the yard tap Lani heard the sound of voices. Looking up, she saw Henry escorting Daniel Blanchett back on to the yard. *Oh rats.* Lani stared over at Honey who had just started to sweep out the loosebox.

Daniel Blanchett raised his eyebrows. "Is it me or are apprentices getting younger?"

Honey turned bright red. "One of the buckets spilled and we thought we'd clean it up," she rushed. She looked apologetically at Henry. "We thought we'd be finished before. . ."

"Before I saw the mess?" Daniel Blanchett finished for her.

Henry winced.

Lani lost her grip on the bucket which clattered on the ground. She watched helplessly as Daniel Blanchett strode over to his car. *If things weren't blown for Henry before, they sure are now.*

Henry looked stricken as the dark blue car pulled away. He closed his eyes briefly before looking down at Honey. "I'd love to know just what went wrong this morning."

"The puppies were shut away, we made sure," Honey promised.

"And yet somehow they managed to get out of a locked loosebox and into a secure chicken run and drag a chicken on to the yard in front of a prospective client?" Henry kept his tone even.

Honey looked wretched. "We don't know how that happened."

"And we don't know how the water bucket was spilled," Dylan chipped in, "but we tried to get it cleaned up before you came back on to the yard."

"Better a small pool of water than giving the impression that I use child labour on the yard," Henry muttered. Lani bit her lip. Henry was right, they shouldn't have tried to clean up. The apology was forming on her lips when Henry sighed. "I'm sorry, Honey," he said, "but I think it's better if you don't come on the yard for a while. I can't afford to do anything to see off more prospective clients."

Lani's stomach twisted. Honey didn't deserve to be banned from the yard. *But then, Henry doesn't exactly deserve this run of bad luck.* She couldn't buy into Dylan's ghost theory but one thing was for sure: everything that could go wrong for Henry at the moment was going wrong. *Just how is he going to turn things around?*

"Oh my gosh." Honey rubbed her fingers against her temples. "Listen to this."

Hearing the ominous tone in Honey's voice, Lani put down her knife and fork. *This isn't going to be good.* She stared at the morning newspaper which Honey had been flicking through.

Honey shook out the paper. "Is the Dysart curse awoken from the grave?" she read aloud. "One may be forgiven for believing that Lord William Dysart, the first of the line of Dysarts, would be more than a little displeased by the estate passing out of the heir's hands – or part of it at any rate. Dysart Home Farm has recently experienced a spate of bad luck that would make even the most unsuperstitious believe in curses. With two of his best runners down, Henry Stilling has his hopes riding on Dardanus, the promising three-year-old by Golden Age. Hope also rests on finding new owners and so nothing worse could occur than one such investor receiving a less than positive impression of the yard."

"How did they find out about yesterday already?" Lani gasped. Honey's eyes met hers briefly before she continued to read.

"With two unfortunate mishaps occurring, one could ask if this was bad luck or poor management. When two puppies sniffed out adventure in the form of an unsecure henhouse, the unlucky chicken became the focus of a tussle in the middle of the yard just as the prospective owner was receiving his tour. Tradition has it that the first Lord Dysart's wrath will awaken if the Dysart estate, or any part of it, passes out of the direct line of descendants. Could it be that Stilling's intent to own the farm has revived the age-old curse?"

Malory drew in a sharp breath. "This is awful! It's bad enough it happened without it being printed all over the local newspaper."

"But who told them?" Dylan exploded.

Lani shook her head. "And then we make things even worse by making it look as if Henry employs underage staff."

Honey sighed. "It's not our fault. We were just trying to help."

The door opened and Meg looked in. "I thought I'd join you for breakfast," she said with a smile. Taking a seat at the table, she looked at each of them. "Is it me or are things less cheerful than one might expect at the start of a glorious spring day?"

Honey sighed and handed Meg the newspaper. The girls were silent as Meg read the article. Finally she folded it and laid it beside her plate. "Dysarts never give in," she said firmly. "You'll see."

"Are you sure Henry won't be mad if he spots us?" Malory asked Honey as they followed her up a twisting worn path.

Honey hesitated, then shook her head. "He banned us from the yard, not the rest of Home Farm."

Lani tilted her face up to the sun, glad that the rain had gone. The air was soft and smelled strongly of cut grass. Her calf muscles ached as the path grew steeper. "No wonder the horses are fit if they have to do this sort of climb every day," she puffed.

Honey glanced over her shoulder. "They don't come up this high. Look." She waited for them to join her in the clearing at the top of the hill, and waved her hand at the view spread out below them.

"Now that's impressive," Lani breathed. From up here, it was possible to see the whole of the Dysart estate, with the racing paddocks closest to them on the flanks of the hill. The gallops were built in two large fields, one of which was circled by an all-weather track made of wood chippings and the other by a course of low brush fences.

"Look!" Malory pointed at the string of racehorses jogging along the trail leading up to the gallops.

Lani admired the way the horses' fluid strides ate up the ground. As they turned to go down to the track, the horses picked up their pace. One by one they broke into a slow canter up the long stretch of grass that led to the all-weather track. Lani leaned forward, trying to work out which of the horses would go around in the fastest time. *Dardanus*. It wasn't a hard choice. The grey gelding's muscles bunched beneath his skin with his eagerness to run.

Out of the corner of her eye, Lani saw a flash of white. Tearing her gaze away from Dardanus, she peered at the end of the course. On the final bend, a sheep was struggling against something that Lani couldn't make out. She stared harder, willing the sheep to break free and get off the course.

"What's that sheep doing?" Dylan said, puzzled.

"I don't know." Lani looked at the horses cantering down to the start of the circuit. "But we'd better get down there fast and find out." Without waiting for the others, she broke into a sprint. She raced down the twisting narrow path, risking a sprained ankle, but all she could think about was getting to the sheep and setting it free before the horses thundered down on it.

"Lani, wait up!" Honey gasped behind her. "Take a right, there's a short cut on to the gallops."

Lani swerved off the path and plunged through waist-high bracken. She burst on to the track a few metres from the stranded sheep. As she ran nearer, she realized what was wrong. A strand of silver barbed wire stretched across the track, the barbs glistening with dew. It wasn't high enough to cause injury to a rider but any horse galloping through it. . . Lani winced.

The wire was tangled deep in the sheep's fleece and the more the animal struggled the more caught up it became. As the others joined her, Lani became aware of the ground vibrating beneath the soles of her trainers.

"The horses are coming! We've got to stop them!" Malory cried.

"I'm on it." Lani leaped over the barbed wire, closely followed by Dylan, and together they raced up the track. "Stop!" Lani yelled and waved her arms.

The lead horse was only a few dozen strides away but the girls stood their ground, flapping at the rider to pull up.

"It's Dardanus!" Dylan shouted as the grey bore down on them.

Lani swallowed hard. She'd heard that a horse would never willingly run down a person but she'd never come so close to putting the theory to the test.

Dardanus' stride faltered and Lani stared up at Wayne.

"Are you crazy? I could have ridden right over you!" Wayne's face was bright red as he turned Dardanus in a tight circle. "Whoa, boy. Steady."

Before Lani or Dylan could explain a large bay gelding loomed up behind Dardanus, eating up the track with loping strides.

"Stop!" Lani yelled. "Wire!"

"Wire?" Wayne echoed as the bay's rider pulled up. *Jess*, Lani realized as the girl struggled to hold back the sweating horse. "Where?"

"On the next bend," Dylan said quickly. "We wouldn't have known it was there but a sheep got caught up in it."

Jess went white. She pulled a whistle out of her jacket pocket with one hand and gave three short bursts. Further down the track, the rest of the string came to a ragged halt. The horses danced and tossed their heads, as if they were cross that their gallop had been interrupted.

"Wire?" Jess repeated incredulously.

"Malory and Honey are trying to take it down," Lani told her. "I think we may need wire cutters."

"I'll phone the yard for some to be brought up." Jess fumbled for her phone.

The other riders trotted towards them. "What's going on?" one of them demanded.

"There's wire on the track," Lani said, but her reply was drowned out by the roar of an engine.

Henry Stilling pulled up on a quad bike. "Why's everyone stopped?" he demanded. Turning to Lani and Dylan, he said furiously, "You have short memories. It was only yesterday I told you to stay off the yard."

Lani bit her lip. She suspected that now wasn't the best moment to point out they weren't technically on the yard.

"Lani thinks there's wire on the track," Wayne interrupted. "If she's right then she may have just saved Dardanus from a bad accident."

Lani shot him a grateful look. "It's definitely wire," she said.

"There's a sheep tangled up in it," Dylan interjected.

The colour drained from Henry's cheeks. "Where?" he said curtly.

Lani pointed down the track. "On the next bend."

"Take the horses back to the yard," Henry told the riders. "Now!"

"Becky's on her way up with wire cutters," Jess said as the riders turned the horses around. She called over her shoulder, "You might have to call out a vet if the sheep is hurt."

Henry waved his hand distractedly before pulling back the throttle on the quad. The engine growled as Henry rode up the track, bumping and rocking over the wood chippings. Lani and Dylan sprinted after him. By the time they rounded the bend Henry was off his quad and kneeling beside Malory and Honey. He grunted with effort as he tried to lift the sheep to stop the wire biting into its neck. "Can you try to get it free?" he hissed.

Lani crouched down and braced herself under the sheep's haunches to try and share its weight with Henry. The sheep scrabbled and kicked against her with surprisingly sharp little hooves. "Steady," she panted. "Hold on, help's coming."

It seemed ages before a Land Rover pulled up. Becky jumped out and hurried over with the cutters. "Try to hold it still," she instructed as she knelt between Malory and Honey. "The wire has gone in really deep."

Lani wrapped her arms around the sheep's flanks, willing it to keep still. Her arms burned with effort.

"I'm really sorry!" Becky gasped. "But I can't see what I'm doing through the wool and I'm scared I'll end up cutting the sheep."

"If you don't hurry then it will end up being strangled anyway," Henry puffed.

Becky took a deep breath and tightened her grip on the cutters. "There!" she exclaimed. "It's free."

With a gasp of relief, Lani let go of the fleece. The sheep collapsed to the ground and lay still.

"We need a vet." Malory's voice trembled.

Becky carefully pulled back the broken strands of wire, avoiding the deadly barbs. "Help me lift the sheep into the back of the Land Rover. I'll drive it down to the yard. Henry, can you call the vet?"

Henry fished out his phone. He spoke briefly before snapping it closed. "She's on her way."

Between them they lifted the sheep into the Land Rover and then the girls jumped inside. They drove back in silence. Lani felt stunned. The barbed wire could have caused a fatal accident to a horse galloping full out. How on earth did it end up stretched across the track like that? She hadn't seen any barbed wire on the farm before now, just immaculate post-and-rail fencing or hedgerows.

Becky pulled up on the yard. "I'm going to see if there's a free stall to put the sheep in." She hurried down to the bottom row of stables, pausing to exchange a brief word with the group of riders standing in the yard.

"I guess we should stay here since we're still officially banned." Lani broke the silence.

Dylan exhaled slowly. "So, does everyone still think that the Dysart Curse hasn't been awoken?"

Malory shook her head. "I've never heard of a ghost stringing barbed wire across a racetrack."

"But that means someone put the wire there deliberately!" Lani whispered.

Honey pushed her hair back from her face. "Can you imagine what would have happened if the horses hadn't been stopped?"

Feeling sick, Lani pressed her hand against her stomach. "Who would do something like that?"

"It could have been children messing about," Malory said, though she didn't sound convinced. "They may not have thought how major the consequences would be."

Lani raised her eyebrows. "And the puppies escaping, and the water buckets being kicked over, and the newspaper article?"

"There are too many coincidences for it to be just a run of bad luck," Honey agreed. Her eyes were wide as she looked around her friends. "If you ask me, someone's out to ruin Henry!"

"Come in!" Henry called.

The girls walked into the office, which was attached to the farmhouse in a single storey red-brick extension. Light poured in through the windows facing the yard. Henry's desk was positioned directly underneath them. He turned in his chair to face the girls. "Sit down." He waved his hand at the small circular table in the middle of the room. "Sorry about the mess." The table was covered in old copies of *The Racing Post* and race schedules.

Lani gently pushed a tabby cat off her chair before sitting down. Nearly every inch of wall space was taken up with photographs and framed pictures of racehorses. Her gaze settled on one of Dardanus in the winners' enclosure. Henry was standing on one side of the gelding and Meg on the other, their faces wreathed with smiles.

Henry followed Lani's gaze. "If you girls hadn't discovered that wire then Dandy's racing days would be finished." He rubbed his hands over his face and Lani felt a stab of sympathy at how strained the trainer looked. "Tell me again how you found it," Henry said. "I'm going to have to inform the police."

Lani took a deep breath. "We'd gone to watch the horses gallop. We watched them ride on to the track and then out of the corner of my eye I saw something moving at the end of the course. Although I couldn't see the wire, I saw the sheep struggling like crazy."

"And because it was on a bend we knew that the riders wouldn't see anything until it was too late," Dylan added.

Malory nodded. "We could see it because we were high up, looking down on the course."

"We raced down to the track and Mal and I tried to help the sheep while Lani and Dylan stopped the horses," Honey finished.

"You did really well." Henry leaned back in his chair. "Without you, goodness knows how many of the string would have been injured. With Colonel and Lucky out of the running, I'd have had no potential Group One winners left to race this season." He looked rueful. "I shouldn't have told you not to come on the yard. You'll have to forgive me but my nerves are rather raw at the moment! You're welcome anytime, of course."

He got up and solemnly shook each of their hands. As he reached Honey he gently ruffled her hair. "Thank goodness you came home when you did!"

Becky looked around the door. "The vet's treated the sheep and given it a sedative. She said that it will need a few days to recover but it's going to be fine."

Henry nodded. "I'm going to arrange for extra security on the yard during the night, and for the gallops to be inspected before any of the horses use them."

Feeling sombre, Lani followed the girls out of the office. *Poor Henry.* They headed down the tiled passage that led to an outside door. Lani patted her pockets and realized she'd left her mobile on the table. "I'll catch up with you guys," she told them.

She retraced her footsteps and hesitated outside the study door as she heard Henry speaking to Becky. "If Dardanus doesn't race at the end of the week then I'm finished." His voice was flat.

"Surely things aren't that bad?" Becky sounded horrified.

Henry sighed. "The racing world is superstitious, Becks. Word's going round that it's bad luck to be associated with Dysart Farm. If I can't get Dardanus to run, and run well, at the next race then no one's going to want to put their horses with me. I took two phone calls yesterday from owners wanting to take their horses off the yard after that newspaper ran its story. If news leaks out about the wire, I'll probably lose all of my owners." His voice sounded muffled as if he had placed his head in his hands. "Things have to turn round for us soon, or we'll be forced to give up."

Lani quietly walked away from the study. She could get her phone later. She couldn't bear seeing Henry and Becky in distress over the possibility of losing their yard and their livelihood.

8

"I've just had to do battle with an entire hothouse of flowers!" Dylan proclaimed. She collapsed on the four-poster bed and fanned herself dramatically.

"Did you get the orchid?" Meg looked up from where she was teasing Malory's dark curly hair into ringlets.

Dylan groaned. "I knew I'd gone downstairs for something."

"I'll go." Honey rolled her eyes. "This party has turned Dylan's brain to mulch."

"Gotcha!" Dylan grinned as she produced a violet flower from behind her back. She handed it over to Meg who carefully pinned it above Malory's ear. Malory stood up and gazed at her reflection. She twirled around, making the blue silk skirt fan out. The colour was a perfect match with Malory's eyes, Lani thought. Her friend looked stunning.

"Beautiful!" Meg smiled in the mirror at Malory. "Right, who's next?"

"Not me." Lani carefully rolled up one leg of her tights so she could slip her foot into it without risking a ladder. "I'm so not ready." She glanced at the dress that was hanging off the wardrobe door. Meg had brought it with her for the first time today and Lani couldn't be sure it would even fit.

Dylan took Malory's place in front of the dressing table. "You are an absolute genius with hair, Meg."

Meg laughed. "With three older sisters always taking up my mother and her maid's attention, I had to learn to manage for myself! So," she began to brush Dylan's red shoulder-length hair, "how are things coming along downstairs?"

"I think you'd call it organized chaos," Dylan reported. "The caterers have taken over the kitchen and dining room. The florists have invaded the ballroom and hall and the groundsmen are everywhere wrestling with ladders and fairy lights."

"You make it sound like a war zone," Honey commented.

Meg sighed happily. "Actually, it sounds like the beginning of every other party we've held here. I'm so glad you girls came and gave us an excuse to hold another do. It's been ages since we've had the house full of young people enjoying themselves."

Lani felt a rush of excitement. After all of the worry at the yard, it was good to think of a night spent partying. Having put on her tights she went to help rescue Honey who was struggling with the laces on the back of her red Madame Gres dress. The dress had a simple classic cut with a heart-shaped bodice, and the skirt fell down to Honey's knees in a waterfall of silk.

"You look amazing," Lani told her.

"Thanks." Honey's eyes shone with excitement. "Now let me help you into yours." She lifted Lani's dress down and slipped it off the hanger. Lani stared at the silver flapper dress for a moment before taking a deep breath and letting Honey pull it over her head. The spaghetti-strapped sequined bodice skimmed over her hips before falling into a tiered skirt. Delicate lace covered the skirt, weighed down with glass teardrops. As Lani turned round so that Honey could zip her up, she caught sight of her reflection in the mirror. *Is that really me?* She looked as if she'd stepped off a 1920s movie set!

Meg clapped her hands in delight. "It suits you perfectly. I knew you needed something that shouted fun but gorgeous, something that was quite unique. That was when I remembered my friend's grandmother who had the most adorable flapper dress. She stole the limelight the night she wore it!"

"There's no way my brother's going to be able to blank you tonight," Honey said quietly. "You look totally stunning."

Meg draped a string of polished black art deco beads over Lani. "You do look absolutely divine," she agreed. "And that's without me having done your make-up and hair! My grandson will be smitten, I'd lay a bet on it!"

Lani bit her lip. She sure hoped so. *Although I can't guarantee the reception he'll get, considering he's barely said a word to me all week.*

Honey giggled. "I'd never risk betting against you, Meg. Have you ever lost?"

Meg's eyes danced, making her look young and playful. "Occasionally at poker, but only to lull the person I'm playing against into a false sense of security." She beckoned Lani over to the dressing table to have her hair done. "With Dardanus running next week, I hope my winning streak doesn't fail. I won't tell you how much I've staked on him to win!"

"You won't be able to do much with it," Lani said apologetically, touching her dark hair.

Meg tipped her head on one side. "I think I just may have something." She used tongs to flatten Lani's hair straight back before hunting through a jewellery roll. Taking out six pins, she carefully slid them into Lani's hair, pinning her fringe into place. Lani caught her breath. At the end of each pin was an exquisite diamond butterfly.

"Now your make-up," Meg said. "This is so much fun!" She applied a kohl outline to Lani's eyes, slanting it slightly to give her a feline look. Taking a blusher brush, she swept light powder up Lani's high cheekbones to leave a dusting of shimmering gold. Finally she rolled on a subtle lip gloss and then stood back. "You're all ready to go and break some hearts!"

Only one heart necessary, Lani thought as she slipped on her sandals. *And while breaking's not on the agenda, melting sure is!*

Honey's family was waiting for them out on the galleried landing. Music floated up, mingled with the sound of guests' conversation and laughter.

Honey's aunt and mother looked beautiful in their ballgowns. As the girls walked towards them, Honey's uncle, looking dashingly handsome in his tuxedo, offered his arm to Amy. "Time for our grand entrance," he teased.

"Sam can walk me down, you walk with Meg," Amy said to her husband. She stood aside for Meg to take her place.

"This takes me back." Meg looked as if she could have been a film star alongside Joan Crawford or Bette Davis, Lani thought. She wore a black sheath of silk with diamante stitched on to the bodice. Diamond earrings caught the light as she tipped back her head and laughed at something Lord Timothy said.

Feeling Sam's eyes on her, Lani turned and met his gaze. Sam coloured and turned away, offering his arm to Amy. *He has to acknowledge me at some point*, Lani thought with a surge of frustration. *He can't let me fly back home without talking things through.*

A smattering of applause broke out as Meg and Lord Timothy appeared at the head of the stairs. The girls paired up and followed the others down the staircase. Tiny white lights had been woven through foliage and around the banister. Lani felt as if she had stepped into a fairy story. Below them, the guests were assembled in the entrance hall. A fire blazed in the hearth, giving off a strong aroma of apple which mixed headily with the scent from the two flower stands positioned at the bottom of the staircase.

Wow, Meg and Amy must have invited every family in the county! Lani tried to take in every detail of the crowded hall. She was determined to imprint the moment in her memory for ever. Underneath the glittering chandelier, the women's dresses created a kaleidoscope of colour. As the string quartet struck up a new melody, waiters stepped forward with plates of canapés and sparkling soft drinks. Lani picked up a glass and raised it.

"To Honey's homecoming! Am I allowed to wish life wasn't quite so good here so you'd change your mind and come back to Chestnut Hill with us?"

Honey reached out to hug her. "Don't think I haven't wished I could be in two places at the same time," she said fervently.

Looking over Honey's shoulder, Lani saw Sam staring at her again. Quickly he turned and struck up a conversation with another boy his age. Lani suppressed a sigh as she decided to ignore his behaviour. *After all, this is supposed to be a party!* She selected a salmon croustade from a waitress and bit into it. Savouring the lemon-scented twist, she wandered over to say hello to Henry and Becky.

"How's the sheep?" she asked. It had been up on its feet when she'd looked in on it that morning during a quick visit to the yard, but she wanted to know if the vet had been called back.

Becky's lips twitched. "That must be the most original greeting I've received at one of Amy's balls!"

Seeing the humour in Becky's eyes, Lani laughed. "You'll have to forgive me if my manners don't quite match up to British etiquette," she said in her deepest drawl.

To her surprise Henry chuckled. "But they're far more refreshing," he said gallantly. "And to answer your question, the sheep is fine. We'll be returning it to its field tomorrow – after the boundaries have been double checked!"

"Lani!" Meg walked up and linked arms with her. "I want you to come and meet some old friends of mine. Their daughter is due to fly out to Colorado this summer to spend some time on a working ranch. They'd like you to put their mind at rest that she won't be in any danger!"

"Would that be from the blizzards, floods, droughts, or mosquitoes?" Lani asked innocently.

Meg's eyes twinkled. "That's my girl! Although maybe you could downplay the danger a little? Lady Harriet is prone to hysterics and I don't have my smelling salts to hand."

A short while later the hum of conversation was broken by Tom announcing that dinner was served. Honey's uncle and Meg led the guests through into the dining room. Lani looked around for Honey and the others and saw them waiting for her alongside the dining room entrance. As they turned to head into the room a male voice rang out, "Of course, it's clearly a fake."

Honey spun around and stared at the ginger-haired man who was examining an oil painting on one of the panelled walls. "That's no fake," she told him. "It's a genuine Gainsborough."

The plump man drew himself up. "I can understand why you would think so. It is, I accept, a very clever copy. You'd have to be an expert to see the flaws." He tapped his nose, as if to underline the fact that he was an expert and Honey was nothing more than an ignorant child.

Honey's cheeks flushed red. "It's been verified by three independent experts after extensive testing, actually. I'd put more trust in their results than your opinion given in poor light!"

Lani had never heard her friend's English accent sound so clipped. Lani slipped her arm through Honey's. "And breathe," she murmured.

Honey shook her head. "Sorry," she said as she walked into the dining room. "I shouldn't have let that get to me. It's just that the painting is Aunt Amy's pride and joy and to hear a guest insulting it goes against the grain."

"Believe me," Dylan chuckled. "He won't dare insult anything else for the rest of the evening. You even had me scared!"

"Wow," Lani murmured. "This sure is some party." The huge oval dining table was set out with startlingly shiny silver cutlery and pristine white plates. Four serving staff were poised to fill guests' glasses. The rest of the room was taken up with circular tables each holding a pair of candelabra.

"We're over there," Honey pointed at a table laid for six. Sam was already seated alongside a boy with dark red hair.

Dylan gave a low appreciative whistle. "Who's Sam's friend?"

"That's our cousin, Will," Honey said. "Aunt Amy's son. His boarding school has different holiday dates from ours so he's only just broken up."

Dylan turned to Malory. "I don't have any spinach stuck in my teeth, do I?"

Malory shook her head. "You're all clear."

Dylan put on her most brilliant smile as she sashayed over to the table.

"Do you think we should have told her about the toilet paper stuck to her shoe?" Lani raised her voice so Dylan would hear her.

Dylan faltered and glanced down. Seeing nothing, she looked over her shoulder and poked her tongue out at Lani.

Lani giggled. "Not at all ladylike. She'll never secure a proposal from an aristocrat acting like that!"

At the table alongside theirs, Lord Timothy stood up and tapped his spoon against his glass. The girls quickly slipped into their seats as silence fell over the room. "Firstly I'd like to thank you all for coming here tonight to celebrate the homecoming of my sister-in-law, brother-in-law, niece and nephew." He glanced over and smiled at Honey and Sam as the guests cheered. "I'd like you to raise your glasses and toast to their future happiness back on English soil and also extend a welcome to Honey's and Sam's American friends who are here on a visit." He raised his glass. "I think they're finding it as hard to let go of Honey and

Sam as we did when they left to make America their home!"

Too right, Lani thought as the guests pushed back their chairs and raised their glasses. "To old friends and new," they echoed after Lord Timothy.

As the serving staff brought in the first course, a Roquefort tart with a walnut side salad, Dylan gave a happy sigh. "I vote we come back in the summer for an extended visit."

"And Christmas," Lani agreed as she picked up the surprisingly heavy knife and fork.

Honey laughed. "Why go back at all?"

Lani glanced at Sam, waiting for him to second the invitation. There was a brief pause before Will said, "Well, if all American girls look as great as you, then I think I'll be looking to enrol across the Atlantic!"

"You forgot to mention our amazing personalities and sparkling wit," Dylan pointed out with a grin.

"Ah, you spotted my deliberate mistake. I thought by omitting them you'd work extra hard to impress me over dinner." Will's green eyes sparkled with humour.

Malory leaned over to murmur in Lani's ear, "I think Dylan may finally have met her match."

"In more ways than one," Lani said softly. She bit into the Roquefort tart and savoured the strong creamy flavour. *I have to remember every detail to tell everyone back home.* Dylan had her digital camera and was on her way to filling up its entire memory card. *I can't wait to see Lynsey's face when she looks at the pictures!*

*

"So what happened to the famous sparkling wit?" Will asked as he dipped and swayed to the music.

"I'm too busy concentrating on not mangling your feet," Lani confessed. "Oops, sorry."

Will winced. "I should have put on my steel toecaps!"

"Hey, I was doing all right until you distracted me," Lani protested.

The music came to an end and everyone clapped before Will walked with Lani back to the edge of the ballroom floor. "I'd love to dance with you later once my toes have recovered," he said with a wink.

"Yes, but I may not want to dance with you," Lani shot back. "I thought English gentlemen were supposed to have better etiquette than to draw attention to their partner's shortcomings."

"I don't believe I called your dancing a shortcoming." Will dipped his head. "And even if it was, I'd still come back to enjoy a dance with one of the best looking girls in the room." He grinned. "Am I forgiven?"

Lani couldn't help her lips twitching with amusement. "Only *one* of the best looking? You'll be forgiven when I'm elevated to the top of the list."

Will held out his hands in a helpless gesture. "And show favouritism among you and your best friends? Think where that might lead. You may all end up fighting and I couldn't be responsible for that."

Lani gave a short shout of laughter. "You have a majorly high opinion of yourself."

Before Will could respond, Dylan hurried up. "Isn't this our dance?"

Will shot Lani an apologetic glance as Dylan tugged him on to the dance floor. *If ever there was a match made in heaven*, Lani thought, watching them whirl around. *It so sucks that they'll soon be a zillion miles apart.* She felt touched by sadness as she glanced across at Sam who was deep in conversation with another boy. It shouldn't be Will she was dancing and laughing with. *It should be Sam.*

As the music ended the band struck up a quickstep which none of the girls knew the steps for. Honey, Dylan and Malory came to stand with Lani. "Will and I have swapped email addys," Dylan said, looking flushed. "I wonder if he could get a student exchange with someone at St Kit's?"

Before anyone could respond, a familiar voice sounded close by. "Lady Amy, what a wonderful evening you've arranged for us."

Glancing over her shoulder Lani saw the stout ginger-haired man who had insulted the Gainsborough earlier that night.

"Thank you, Julian," Amy said. "I'm glad you're having a good time."

"Oh, marvellous," he replied in booming tones. He tapped his nose again, like he was punctuating his own sentences. "I've especially enjoyed admiring your collection of oil paintings."

Dylan took a quick indrawn breath. "What a snake," she said in disgust.

Lani couldn't help agreeing.

Honey shrugged. "I've never seen him before so it's

not like he's a close friend of the family. Let's hope tonight's a one-off invitation."

"So," Honey slipped her arm through Lani's, "I haven't seen you and Sam dancing yet."

Lani felt her cheeks burn.

"Have you guys fallen out?" Dylan asked. "Is that why Sam's avoiding you?"

Before Lani could respond Honey said, "Hasn't Sam spoken to you at all tonight?" She sounded stunned.

Lani hesitated. There was no way she wanted to spoil Honey's homecoming ball by telling her Sam was still giving her the brush-off.

"But you look a million dollars!" Malory cried. Her eyes were bright. "How can he ignore you like this?" Dylan laid a warning hand on Malory's arm. Looking at Honey's startled expression, Malory bit her lip and stared at the floor.

Lani's stomach twisted. "It's not a problem," she heard herself saying. "We've arranged to talk things through after the ball."

"Really?" Hope animated Honey's expression.

"Really." Lani crossed her fingers behind her back. Now that she'd said so, she'd have to force Sam to speak with her.

I'll have to do it ASAP. The others are going to want to know exactly what's going on before we set foot on the plane home. And so do I, for that matter.

Lani went down to breakfast the next morning, determined to speak to Sam before she forgot how rude he had been last night by acting as if she wasn't there.

Mrs Harper was stirring her cup of coffee. "You're up early, considering how late you went to bed last night," she said with a smile.

"The others are still in bed," Lani admitted, not wanting to confess that the only reason she was up was to catch Sam. She looked about and realized that all traces of the party had been cleared away.

"The catering staff didn't leave until the early hours," Mrs Harper told her. "They did a great job." She took a sip of her coffee. "Did you enjoy the party?"

"It was amazing." Lani sat down at the table and poured herself an orange juice. Taking a piece of toast from the silver rack, she spread butter on it before asking ultra casually, "Has Sam had breakfast yet?"

"He and Will went back with a friend of theirs last night," Mrs Harper said.

Lani's heart sank. She'd got herself psyched up to

confront Sam and now she'd have to put it all on hold again.

"By the way, this arrived today." Mrs Harper pushed over a plate which held a postcard. "It's addressed to all you girls."

Feeling curious, Lani picked up the card which had a picture of rolling forested mountains on the front. Turning it over, she exclaimed, "It's from Mr O'Neil and Ms Carmichael!" Malory's dad and Dylan's aunt had recently started dating but Lani didn't know they'd had plans to go away for Spring Break.

Mrs Harper smiled. "I'll leave you to it while I go to wake the girls. We thought we'd take you into Oxford today."

Lani's spirits lifted at the prospect of a trip into the university city that had been special enough to draw Mr Harper back from his teaching post in the States. *It's going to be a great day and I'm not going to let stressing out about Sam ruin it*, she thought as she returned her attention to the postcard.

Dear Mal, Dylan, Lani and Honey,
    Greetings from the Ozarks! We decided, very spur of the moment, to see if we could go away for a short break and found an amazing deal to visit the Ozarks. We've walked and climbed every day and seen a few endangered species. Today we're going to visit Sly Mill, a grist and saw mill on Spring River in the Springfield Plateau. We hope you're all having a wonderful time in England

and can't wait to catch up with you at the end of
Spring Break.
Hugs,
Karl (Dad) and (Aunt) Ali.

Lani smiled as she set the card back down for the others to read. *Mal and Dyl will be stoked.* She finished her toast before pushing back her chair. She'd miss going to the yard today but couldn't wait to hit the streets of Oxford!

"There's Jesus College." Honey pointed to an imposing gateway beyond which was a building of golden stone built around a lawn-covered courtyard. "It's where Dad will be teaching."

Oxford was even more beautiful than Lani had imagined. The skyline was filled with steeples and spires rising up from the ancient buildings, and each college seemed like an oasis of quiet in the busy modern city. The walls were covered with soft purple wisteria or glossy green ivy, and students hurried around, looking very serious behind their armfuls of books.

"Honey, how about you show the others around and your dad and I will meet up with you at our favourite teashop in an hour?" Mrs Harper suggested.

"OK," Honey agreed, waving them off. She slipped her arm though Lani's. "If you would like to follow me, ladies, I shall be your guide for your tour of Oxford. If you look to your left, you will see the Bodleian Library, which is a copyright library meaning it receives a copy of every single book that is in print. The buildings you see here are much smaller than the floors below ground known as the Stack, which is where the majority of books are stored."

A middle-aged couple holding guides to the city gave them a quizzical look.

Lani giggled. "If you're not careful, you'll have people paying to tag along!" She gazed at the coats-of-arms painted on the double oak doors before craning her neck to stare up at the gothic knotwork on the magnificent building. "How long do you figure it took to be built?"

Dylan shook her head. "More to the point, how do you figure they built it to last hundreds and hundreds of years?"

Honey showed them across Radcliffe Square, flanked on one side by the library and the other by St Mary's Church, with its tall spire that seemed to graze the fluffy white clouds. In the centre of a lawn inside the square stood a neat domed building called the Radcliffe Camera. The circular building's central tier had pillars carved into it supporting an ornate balcony.

"Radcliffe Camera is a library that was funded by a legacy left by Dr John Radcliffe," Honey told them. "It's part of the Bodleian Library and is linked to the main buildings by an underground tunnel!"

Lani was distracted by a group of students walking by, having an animated debate. Caught up in the atmosphere of learning, she suddenly had an overwhelming desire to come and study at Oxford when she graduated from Chestnut Hill.

Honey tugged her arm. "Come on, I want to show you one of my favourite places." She led them out of the square and along a street which had a pretty roofed-in bridge connecting two buildings. "It's called the Bridge of Sighs," Honey told them, "even though it's nothing like its Venetian namesake!" The bridge formed a perfect arc over the road. With its mullioned windows and carved cherubs, it looked ancient and romantic. "Don't be fooled," Honey warned. "It was only built in the last century."

"I've never been anywhere so amazing in all my life," Malory sighed as Honey led them down Broad Street, a wide pedestrian-only thoroughfare flanked by colleges on one side and cute sandwich shops and tourist stores on the other. "You're so lucky to have all this on your doorstep."

Honey gave a small smile. "I'd rather be with you guys," she said with a touch of sadness.

"Hey!" Lani broke the mood. "Did someone mention a teashop earlier?"

"Nice change of subject there, Lani," Dylan told her. "Absolutely seamless."

Lani winked. "I was hoping no one noticed."

"Absolutely not," Dylan teased.

Honey tipped back her head and laughed. "Come on! I feel the need for a chocolate rush!"

They walked down the main shopping street and Honey turned down a narrow road. "Not far now," she promised.

Lani stopped dead in the middle of the pavement

and stared at the spectacular honey-coloured building, topped with a sturdy domed spire and lined with comical gargoyles, each one slightly different. Gatekeepers in raincoats and bowler hats stood in the entrance, raising their hats to students but looking distinctly frosty when tourists tried to enter the college.

"That's Christ Church," Honey told her. "It's something else, isn't it?"

"That's not a church, that's a small city," Dylan told her.

"It's one of the largest colleges in the University," Honey said, "and the dining room was used to film the Harry Potter movies." She pushed open the glass door of a teashop on the opposite side of the street from the college entrance. "Come and take a load off."

Lani had to tear herself away from the sight of Christ Church. How did the students manage to concentrate on their studies in a place that looked like a fantasy movie set? Entering the teashop, she grinned as she was greeted with images from Alice in Wonderland and Through the Looking Glass. The Mad Hatter strolled across the closest wall with his nose in the air, and above her the Cheshire Cat beamed down, his teeth very white against the blue sky.

"Lewis Carroll was a Maths scholar at Oxford," Honey explained as they bagged a table at the window.

Lani picked up the menu, which had a white rabbit checking a stopwatch on it. "I'll have scones and jam, what you guys call an English cream tea, right?"

Honey nodded. "Four cream teas?" she asked the others.

"Count me in," said Dylan.

"I've had an English cream tea but not in England," Malory laughed, "so count me in, too!"

Lani looked out of the window, astonished by the amount of cyclists going by. "I think there's more cyclists than pedestrians," she observed.

"It is the done thing in Oxford," Honey said with a smile. "Every student gets around by bike, because most of the studying is done in buildings quite far from the city centre. Colleges are mostly for living and eating, and weekly meetings with tutors."

Lani's attention was captured by a slight figure across the road with bright blond hair. For a moment she thought it was Sam but when the person turned around she realized that it was Clancy. *What's he doing here?* "Look, guys, it's Clancy," she said. The head lad was talking with a larger man who was wearing a perky tweed hat.

Malory pressed her nose up against the window. "Who's that with him?"

"I don't know, but whoever it is will soon be scared off if you carry on squidging up your face like that," Dylan said with a giggle.

Lani stared at the two men. She was sure that she knew the person Clancy was speaking to but before she could figure out who it was, the men finished their conversation and moved off in separate directions.

"Four cream teas," their waitress announced as she put plates, cups and saucers down on the table.

Lani split open the warm scone and spread

strawberry jam and clotted cream in generous layers. She took a bite of the sweet moist cake and sighed happily. Looking across at Christ Church, which gave off a golden glow in the afternoon sunlight, she decided that this wouldn't be the last time she'd visit Oxford.

One day I'll come back, she promised herself.

Lani tugged up the zip on her yard jacket. "More rain." She leaned her elbows on the loosebox door and stared out over the yard.

"You're not a fair weather rider, are you?" Wayne asked.

"Oh, I'm an all weather rider, without a doubt," Lani said immediately. She spun around. "Any particular reason why you're asking?"

Wayne chuckled. "I'm going to take Dandy out to stretch his legs and I was wondering if you'd like to bring Wichita out to keep us company."

Lani's heart leapt. "The others will be thrilled!"

Wayne raised his hand. "It will just be us, if that's OK. I'm keeping things steady and calm for Dardanus in the lead-up to his race."

Lani hesitated. She would barter her favourite Tahoe chaps for the chance to gallop a genuine racehorse, but how could she leave the others behind on yard duties?

"Jess mentioned taking you all out on the trails." Wayne read her thoughts. "I just thought you might prefer to ride up to the gallops instead. Wichita's a totally safe ride. She's long been retired but we use her as a lead horse to accompany the others."

Almost dancing with excitement, Lani collected Wichita's tack and let herself into the mare's box to tack up. As she buckled up the girth, she felt a rush of nerves. *Steady, cowgirl*, she told herself. *You can handle this.*

Wayne echoed her sentiment as they took the track up to the Downs. "You'll find it easier than you think. All you have to do is take your weight in your stirrups and let her go. She'll look after you. She'll know when she's had enough, too, so let her slow down at her own pace."

Lani patted Wichita's neck. "Are you listening?" Wichita's short black mane bounced against her neck as she walked with a long hurried stride.

As they turned into the first paddock, both horses broke into a trot. Lani glanced at Wayne who was lightly raised in the saddle.

"Grab a handful of mane if you need to find your balance," Wayne called across as Dardanus broke into a canter.

But Lani was already adjusting to the high riding position, letting her weight rest on the balls of her feet and keeping her hands low and still close to the pommel of the saddle. She leaned over Wichita's neck, settling into the mare's rhythmical stride as it became a canter.

"Good, good," Wayne called. "You're doing great!"

Lani grinned. It *felt* great! As they headed across the stretch of grass leading on to the all-weather track, she softened her hands. Wichita stretched out her neck and crouched down on her hindquarters for a sudden burst of speed. Lani's breath caught in her throat at the mare's surge of power. Alongside them, the grey gelding's breath came in loud snorts as he strained to go faster. The ground became a blur as Lani urged Wichita on. Obediently the mare responded, her hooves thundering in a sweet tattoo. Dardanus edged forward, his tail streaming like a banner in the air. Wayne opened him up and the grey gelding pulled away, his muscles bunching and releasing as he flew over the ground.

After they had completed a circuit, Lani felt Wichita begin to slow. Regretfully she allowed the mare to slacken her pace while ahead of them, Dardanus thundered away. Wichita kept to a steady slow gallop and after another circuit Lani pulled her up. "Good girl." She patted Wichita's damp steaming neck. "That was amazing. What a rush!" She trotted Wichita off the track and kicked her feet clear of the stirrups so that she could stretch her legs.

"I thought Colorado had a mean turn of speed but back there even he'd have been eating your dust!" She shook her head in astonishment. "That was unforgettable, absolutely unforgettable."

The earlier showers had turned into a full-scale downpour. Rain drummed against the drawing room's windowpanes as the girls sat around a table playing Scrabble. "C, O, L, O, R." Malory set her counters down on the board. "That makes colour and gives me. . ." She paused as she began counting up her points.

"Hey, you can't do that," Will objected. "You've missed out the letter U."

Malory frowned. "Colour doesn't have a U in it."

"It does when you're in the United Kingdom," Will told her. "When in Rome, etc."

Dylan picked up a cushion and tossed it at him. "You've just given us our first example of a stuffy Brit, with or without a U!"

Will gave an exaggerated frown. "Stuffy without a U? So I guess that makes me stffy."

"It makes you a total nightmare." Dylan groaned.

Lani smiled at their banter but her heart wasn't really in it. Even though the boys had returned a few hours ago, Sam still hadn't put in an appearance. She glanced over at the fire and saw it was burning low. Rather than bother one of the staff to get some logs she decided to go and fetch some herself. "I'll be back in a few minutes," she announced. "I'm going to get some more logs for the fire."

"Do you want me to come with you?" Honey neatly slid the board across the table to avoid the cushion Will had thrown back at Dylan.

"No, I'm good, thanks." Lani stepped out into the hall and grabbed up her jacket.

Once outside she headed over to the disused stable block, aiming for the middle stable which was used as a wood store. She was surprised to see that the doors were already open. Her heart began to pound when she saw

Sam inside. He had his back to her as he swung down an axe to split a log.

Lani hesitated, unsure whether she should slip away before he saw her. *Get a grip*, she told herself. *This is your chance to find out what's bugging him.*

She took a deep breath as Sam kicked the split logs into the main pile. "Hey, Sam," she said, surprised by how calm and controlled her voice sounded.

Sam quickly turned, losing his grip on the axe which clattered to the ground. Sam jumped out of the way and then looked back at Lani, his expression a mixture of wariness and surprise. "Hey." His cheekbones coloured as he glanced down at his watch. "Um, I've got to run. I've got to be somewhere."

Lani felt a rush of anger. Crossing her arms, she refused to move out of the doorway. "Yes, you do have to be somewhere. Right here, talking to me." She shook her head in frustration. "I can't believe you want to walk away. I never had you down as a coward."

Sam held up his hand in protest. "Lani, it's not like that."

"Then tell me what it *is* like." Lani's mouth felt as dry as the sawdust covering the stable floor.

Sam shook his head. "I can't." His voice was hoarse. Lani felt a stab of pain when she saw dampness shining in his eyes. *Had she got this totally wrong?*

"It's not that I don't care," Sam went on. "It's that I..." He broke off and scuffed his foot against the chopping block. "I don't know how to act, knowing that by this time next week there'll be five thousand miles between us," he confessed in a rush.

Lani hesitated. It was something she had wondered about a hundred times since finding out that Sam was leaving the States, as well. At least he was being honest.

"I guess I thought it would be better for the two of us if I backed off," Sam went on. "Maybe we wouldn't miss each other so much if you were already mad at me!" He gave a weak laugh. "I failed, huh?"

"Actually, you nearly succeeded," Lani told him. "I thought you'd changed your mind about me."

Sam looked directly at her. "That's never going to happen," he said quietly.

Lani stepped closer to him. "You're moving back to the UK, not disappearing in a puff of smoke. My mom has this sign in her kitchen that says, 'The heart knows no distance'. When Dad's away, she says it reminds her that just because the person you want to be with is miles away, it doesn't mean you can't think about each other."

"I guess there's email, and Skype, and my dad already said we could get a landline deal with cheap overseas phone calls," Sam said slowly.

Relief flared inside Lani. "It won't be exactly the same, of course it won't, but we can keep in touch every day if we want to. You'll be sick of the sight of my name in your inbox!" She looked up at him, suddenly aware how much he had grown since finishing his last bout of chemotherapy. He had been on eye level with her then, but now she definitely had to tip back her head to look into his face.

"Don't make saying goodbye worse than it has to be," she begged. "We still have some time together. I'd like to go home with happy memories!"

Her heart thudded as Sam reached out and brushed his thumb down her jawline. He dipped his head and pressed his lips against hers in a gentle kiss.

Lani leaned her head on Sam's shoulder. "Let's just focus on what we have now and leave the future to the wonders of international communication. Deal?"

"Deal," Sam agreed. After a moment he released her, his face suddenly animated. "Come on," he told her. "Let's go for a walk."

"It's raining!" Lani protested, laughing.

"You call this rain?" Sam teased as he headed out of the stable. He spun around, holding his hands up to the sky. "It's not even drizzle." He reached into the stable and grabbed Lani's hand.

"You're crazy!" Lani shrieked as the rain beat down.

Sam slipped his arm around her waist and held her hand in his. "We never had a dance at the homecoming ball, did we?"

"I believe that was because you were so ungallantly ignoring me, sir," Lani said in her best imitation of an English accent.

"Allow me to make up for it," Sam said. "I'll do a much better job of it than Will, I promise." He whirled her around.

"Much as I'd love to put the blame on Will, I have to

'fess up that it was me doing the toe crunching," Lani said breathlessly.

"I won't feel a thing," Sam promised her. "I'm wearing Wellington boots!"

Tunelessly he began to hum the Viennese waltz. Lani moved with him in a one, two, three beat, trying to resist the urge to watch her feet.

"Well?" Sam raised an eyebrow at her as they made their second lap of the yard.

"It's OK," Lani told him. "But the orchestra sucks."

Sam looked indignant. "You can do any better?"

In response, Lani began to sing the chorus of Kelly Clarkson's *"My life would suck without you"*, punctuated by giggles and sniffs as raindrops collected on the end of her nose. As they dipped and spun around the courtyard, she thought she'd never been so happy and sad at the same time. She gazed at Sam, seeing the raindrops glistening on his eyelashes, the sparkle of humour in his blue eyes, his lips stretched in a broad smile. She knew she'd remember this moment for ever.

"Enough dancing?" Sam asked as Lani's voice petered out.

Lani would never have enough dancing with him but she nodded her head. "Uh huh."

Sam slipped his hand through hers. "OK, let's have our walk."

As they headed around the back of the house, the rain eased to a fine drizzle and the sun shone through a break in the clouds. They walked down a flight of steps into a paved sunken garden. "I learned to ride my bike here," Sam told Lani. He pointed at the stone shrub-filled troughs that symmetrically lined the garden. "If you look more closely you'll see the cracks where I kept crashing."

"So you were as lame at riding a bike as you are at playing baseball?" Lani gasped.

"Hey, I'm opening up to you here." Sam sounded injured. "And all you can do is mock?"

"OK." Lani smiled. "Tell me some more and I promise I won't make fun."

In the centre of the garden was a large ornamental fishpond. "This," Sam said, "was where I got my first swimming lesson."

Lani couldn't hold back a shout of laughter. "With your bike?"

"With my bike," Sam said ruefully. "And you promised not to laugh!" He gave her hand a quick squeeze. "Come on. I'll show you where Honey and I built a den. It was a work of art. We even managed to get two old armchairs inside!"

They walked out of the walled garden and headed across a lawn which swept down to a lake. Fringing the lake were weeping willows, their branches trailing lightly on the water. As they walked towards the trees, Lani stole a glance at Sam. *He really has come home*, she acknowledged with a bittersweet rush of emotion. *This is where he and Honey truly belong.*

The shrill ring of the alarm clock woke Lani. Lying in the darkness she wondered why she felt so happy. Then it came to her. *Sam!* Yesterday they had taken the bikes and gone for a picnic on the Downs together. It had been as if the previous week had never happened.

Lani pressed her arm over her eyes as light flooded the room. "Why are you guys just lying there?" Dylan demanded as she hauled back the curtains. "It's race day!"

Reason number two for happy rush, Lani thought as she pushed back the covers. They were driving over to Newbury Racecourse later on to watch some of the novice horses run. Tomorrow was Dardanus' big day when he would run in the Classic Cup. Lani felt a shiver of excitement as she thought of seeing the horses race. She grabbed up her yard clothes and beat Dylan to the bathroom by a nanosecond.

"No fair!" Dylan shouted through the door.

"That will teach you for lazing in bed!" Lani called back.

"Lazing in bed?" Dylan spluttered. "I was trying to drag Malory out of it!"

With a grin, Lani splashed water on her face before pulling on her clothes. As soon as she was ready she headed downstairs closely followed by the others.

They had arranged to eat breakfast in the kitchen. Sally stood at the range with bacon sizzling in a pan. "Morning," she said without looking round.

"This is as big as the common room back at school," Lani commented, admiring the high-ceilinged room with its freestanding dressers and units. Tempting smells filled the air as the girls sat down at a long oak table which looked as if it had survived a hundred years of hard scrubbing.

Sally carried over warm plates. "I'll dish up in a few minutes," she said with a glance at the clock above the fireplace. "Then I'll drive you over to the yard as soon as you've finished."

"That's great, thanks, Sal," Honey said appreciatively.

As soon as they had eaten their bacon and eggs the girls headed out to Sally's car. "Sorry," Sally apologized as the engine turned over, refusing to kick into life. "It's never a great starter in the cold."

"My mom's car's just the same," Lani said. She clapped her hands together. "OK, listen up. Everyone out, except for Sal." She jumped out of the car and looked back in. "We'll push you and once you're rolling pop the car."

"Pop the car?" Sally laughed. "That's a new one on me!"

"Let's do this!" Lani called.

The girls braced themselves against the bright red Mini and pushed. Slowly it rolled down the gravel driveway. Once it was picking up speed Sally slipped it into gear and turned the key. The engine roared into life and Lani let out a whoop.

Sally stopped and kept the engine running while the girls scrambled in. "Let's hope the horses are less temperamental," she said with a laugh as she released the handbrake.

It's not the horses we've got to worry about, Lani thought, feeling a shiver run down her spine. *It's whoever's got it in for Henry.*

Lani had never seen the yard so busy. Parked up in the centre was a huge horse truck with its ramp down and gates open. Stable lads were carrying in hay nets and buckets while Clancy inspected the tyres. He smiled when he saw the girls. "I wasn't sure if you'd be able to peel yourselves out of bed this morning."

"Oh, it was no problem." Malory's lips twitched as Dylan shot her an accusing glance.

"What shall we help with?" Honey asked.

"Jess is down in the tack room, I'm sure she'd appreciate a hand bringing it up on to the lorry," Clancy told her before returning his attention to the truck.

As they walked down to the lower block one of the horses raised its head and let out a piercing whinny. One of the stable lasses rolled her eyes. "Sweetie knows it's a race day and she's reminding me that she mustn't be left behind," she explained. As she neared the loosebox, the grey mare's ears flashed back and she snapped bad-temperedly at the girl.

"Wow, Sweetie by name but most definitely not by nature," Malory observed.

"Her racing name's Seal Morning," Honey told her. "But I agree, it's not the most accurate of stable names!"

They headed into the tack room where Jess was counting out saddles and bridles. "Morning, Jess," Honey greeted her. "Clancy said you might want us to carry the tack up to the lorry."

"That would be great," Jess replied. "I'm just about done checking them over. . ." She glanced up as a stable lad came into the room.

"Clancy wants you to come and supervise the loading of the horses."

Jess looked distractedly at the set of tack she was just about to look at. "I'll be up in just a moment."

The stable lad looked awkward. "He was sort of insistent that you came now."

With a sigh Jess headed to the door.

"I guess we should take the tack up," Honey said with a glance at her watch. She lifted up the first of the lightweight saddles and bridles.

Lani scooped up the second set of tack. She packed it into its travel box and turned to follow Honey out of the room.

Behind her Malory said, "What's this?"

Something in her voice made Lani turn. Malory was

bent over one of the saddles. She unbuckled the girth and held it up.

"What?" Dylan peered at the girth. "I don't see anything."

Malory pinched each side of the strap and pulled. Lani gasped as a slash was revealed in the middle of the fabric. "There's no way that would have held during a race."

Malory nodded. "And with the damage being in the middle of the strap, it's unlikely anyone would have seen it."

"It would have been right under the horse's stomach," Honey agreed. She looked at the travelling box. The lid was printed with the name *Seal Morning*. "It was Sweetie's girth!" she exclaimed. "Just about the worst horse on the yard to get a broken girth. She'd have gone nuts."

The girls exchanged worried looks. "Should we tell Henry?" Lani whispered, knowing how close to despair he already was.

Honey hesitated. "Let's tell Clancy. He'll know what to do." She selected a new girth from a shelf and placed it in Sweetie's travel box. "Let's go."

The yard echoed with the sound of metal-shod hooves as Ashdance and Sweetie were led towards the lorry. The girls stashed the tack boxes in a compartment below the lorry and then went over to talk to Clancy.

"Have you got a minute?" Honey asked him.

"Can it wait until later?" Clancy puffed as he jumped up the ramp to close the gates. "If we don't leave now, we'll be running late." He headed back down the ramp where Jess was waiting to help him secure it. "You girls are travelling with Becky."

Honey bit her lip. "OK," she said. "We'll catch up with you at the racecourse."

"We'll have to tell Jess if Clancy's too busy to talk at the racecourse," Dylan said as they hurried down to the farmhouse. "Someone needs to know what we found. There may be other sabotage."

"At least we know Jess has checked the rest of the tack," Honey said. "And we're just going to have to make sure that the horses and tack are watched carefully."

Lani frowned. "We know that someone's out to get Henry, but have you guys realized that it must be someone who works for him?"

Honey's eyes widened. "That's impossible! No one who works here would do that. They're all incredibly loyal!"

Lani pulled a face. The last thing she wanted was to upset Honey. "Maybe I'm wrong," she said.

"What makes you think that it's one of Henry's workers?" Malory pressed.

"Shhh. . ." Honey warned as they headed up the path to the farmhouse. "We'll talk about this later when Becky and Henry aren't around."

Becky was already in the Land Rover and when she saw the girls she started up the engine.

Reg had been talking to her through the driver's window but he stood back as the girls got into the car. "You take care today," he called out as Becky slowly backed the car down the drive. "You don't know what old Lord Dysart's ghost might be planning next!"

Becky shook her head as she drove down the country lane. "He means well," she said. "But it's not really what Henry needs to hear right now. He's anxious enough about race day as it is."

"Where is Henry?" Honey asked.

"He's already left," Becky told her. "He's picking up Meg and driving her down."

"So, how do you think we're going to do today?" Dylan said, as if she was trying to make everyone more positive.

Becky pulled on to the main road before answering. "None of the races are going to be too demanding. They're just five or six furlongs long and most of the runners are making their debut. Sweetie's our most promising outing. The last time I checked, her odds were 9 to 2. Both Ash and Fred are rank outsiders; Ash because it's her debut and Fred because he's been off form in his last couple of outings."

Lani blinked, realizing there was a lot of racing jargon that she needed to get a grip on. Honey was nodding, but Dylan and Malory looked as blank as she felt. *I guess we're heading to the right place to pick up the lingo!*

Honey led the way to the temporary stables, made from pale canvas stretched over wooden frames, where the horses were kept for the day. "Our horses are down here," she said, pointing.

Lani stood back as a tall black gelding was led into

a stable just in front of her. Another lad walked past pushing a bike laden with blankets.

"I never thought I'd see chaos on a grander scale than a Chestnut Hill competition day," Malory said as she sidestepped a group of trainers discussing the race programme.

"There's Mike!" Honey pointed to a slim dark-haired man dressed in a bright-green silk racing shirt. "He's one of Henry's riders." The jockey was talking to Henry outside Ash's stall.

"Her form's sound," Henry was saying as Jess led Ash out. The mare's coat gleamed and her nostrils flared as she stared at her new surroundings. "She really held her own on the gallops yesterday but I'm not sure how she's going to respond to the pressure of her first race."

Mike nodded, his brown eyes serious. "I'll only open her up when she feels settled," he told Henry as he took Ash's saddle. Nodding his head at Honey, he strode off to weigh in.

"Why don't you girls go and find Meg in the owners' enclosure?" Henry said. "Ash is in the first race. I'll be down in a few minutes."

As the girls made their way down to the grandstand, Honey suggested they went past the paddock where they could see the horses being led round before the race. On their way they met Jess hurrying towards them, her cheeks flushed. "The going's softer than we thought and Mike needs his goggles," she puffed.

"I'll get them," Lani offered.

Jess shot her a grateful glance. "Mike thinks he left

them on top of Ash's grooming box," she said. "Can you bring them down to the paddock?"

"I'm already on it." Lani turned and jogged back to the stables. As she turned the corner, she almost crashed straight into Clancy, who was letting himself into Fred's stable with a bucket of water in his hand. He blinked in surprise, and narrowly avoided dropping the bucket.

"I'm just getting Mike's goggles," Lani explained.

"I'm getting a stain out of Fred's coat," Clancy said in return.

Lani paused. Clancy didn't have to explain himself to her. "I know how tough they can be to get out," she told him, thinking of the times Dylan had sweated over getting marks out of Morello's white patches. "Oh, there's something I need to tell you!" She decided to take the opportunity to tell Clancy about the slit girth.

Clancy frowned. "I think you did the right thing by not telling Henry," he said. "Don't worry, I'll make sure we keep a close eye on things today."

Lani spotted Mike's goggles lying on the box outside Ash's stable and scooped them up. "Are you coming to watch Ash run?"

"I'll be there in just a minute," Clancy told her.

"Good," Lani replied. "Team Stilling needs as many fans rooting for it as possible!"

"Come on! The race is about to start!" Honey flapped her hands at Lani to hurry.

Lani joined them in the open-air stand. "Hey, Meg. How's it going?" She smiled at the old lady.

"I'll let you know once this race is over!" Meg said.

Lani stared down at the racecourse, looking for Ash. Some of the horses were fighting their handlers, nervous of entering the row of green cages known as starting stalls. Ashdance was halfway along, and Lani tensed as the mare ran back and reared up in protest. Jess put up her hand to calm her before leading her back to the row of cages.

"Go in, go in," Lani murmured. To her relief Ash allowed herself to be pushed into the stall.

They waited for the last few horses to enter, and a moment later the doors facing the course sprang open. Lani's hands clenched as if she was holding a set of reins. "Come on, Ash!" she urged.

"He's holding her back. Why's he holding her back?" Dylan asked as the distance between the four lead horses and Ash lengthened.

"He'll open her up at the right time," Henry explained without taking his eyes off the runners.

The tannoy rang out above the noise of the crowd. "As they head for home it's Jed Marley on Fool's Gold. In second it's Phoenix Arising struggling to hold his position."

Lani scowled as the jockeys lashed the horses with their whips. "I don't understand why they have to hit them like that."

"Yes, if whips were banned then they'd all be on a level playing field," Malory argued.

Meg's lips twitched. "You make it sound as if they're footballers." She handed her binoculars to Malory. "If you notice, they're barely touching the horses. They're moving the whips back and forth, but aren't making contact most of the time. The racecourse stewards have the power to fine or ban jockeys who leave marks on their horses, so use of whips is very carefully monitored."

Lani's heart thudded as the distance closed between Ash and the fourth horse.

"Ashdance is beginning to open up now in the hands of Mike Anderson," came the commentary over the loudspeaker. "They're in the final furlong, with Fool's Gold out in front. I don't think Ashdance is going to do enough to get past Phoenix Arising."

The two lead horses thundered past the post followed a moment later by Ash. The crowd burst into applause. "Well done, Henry," Meg congratulated him. "That was an excellent outing."

Henry nodded. "She's got real potential."

Lani glanced around for Clancy and frowned as she realized that he hadn't made it to watch Ash run after all. Something niggled at her and as she turned back to look at the jockeys standing up in their stirrups to canter away from the finishing post, she tried to figure what it was. Suddenly it came to her. *Clancy was carrying a black bucket for drinking, not a yellow bucket for washing.* Lani knew that the horses weren't supposed to eat or drink anything before a race because a full stomach would slow them down. It was the same when one of the ponies at Chestnut Hill was taking part in a competition. *And Clancy would know that, too!*

*

Lani carried a coolbox from the back of the Land Rover over to a picnic bench. She kept turning over in her mind what she had seen earlier. *Maybe Clancy just chose the wrong colour bucket by mistake.* She set the coolbox alongside the picnic hamper. *Or maybe I've got it wrong. Maybe it is OK for horses to have a tiny drink of water before they race.*

She sat down between Dylan and Honey.

"Tuck in," Becky invited. "Henry and Meg won't be joining us as they're lunching with some other owners. Henry's hoping it might lead to new horses being put on the yard."

"We'll keep our fingers crossed," Dylan said as she bit into a cream cheese and salmon bagel.

Lani selected a chicken drumstick and held it listlessly over her paper plate. "Becky," she asked in a rush, "is it all right for horses to be offered a drink of water before they race?"

Becky shook her head. "No way. It's a golden rule that they must never eat or drink. Even half a bucket of water would slow them down or make them pull up."

Lani nodded. *Maybe Clancy got the buckets mixed up, then.* But deep down she couldn't believe that the head lad would choose the wrong bucket to wash Fred down. *Could it be Clancy who's trying to ruin Henry?* It was such an awful thought that she tried to push it away. But as she bit into the chicken, the small voice in her head persisted. *Clancy's in the perfect situation to sabotage Henry. Everyone trusts him and he can arrange things just how he wants on the yard. . .*

"Earth to Lani." Honey clicked her fingers in front of Lani's face. "Where've you gone?"

Lani blinked. "Sorry, guys. What did I miss?"

Becky smiled. "I asked what you thought of the race?"

"Amazing," Lani said. "I never thought I could get interested in horses running in a straight line."

"You'd need to throw in some barrels to make it interesting for Lani." Dylan grinned.

Lani nodded ruefully. "It's true! But from the moment they came out of the stalls I was hooked."

"I think knowing Ash gave the race an extra edge," Malory said.

"Talking of which, when's our next race?" Honey asked.

Becky glanced at her watch. "In twenty minutes, so eat up!"

As the horses cantered down to the starting stalls, Lani glanced at Henry and Meg. Seeing them intent on watching the line-up, she whispered to Honey, "I saw Clancy going into Fred's stable earlier with a bucket of water."

Honey frowned. "That doesn't mean he was going to give it to Fred to drink."

"It was in a black bucket," Lani told her.

Honey's frown deepened. "Clancy's worked with Henry for years. He wouldn't do anything to hurt any of the horses, or to damage Henry's reputation."

Lani sighed. It didn't make much sense to her either. But so far it was all she had to work with.

The horses sprang out of the stalls and galloped down the course. Lani watched Just Fred's every move, waiting to see him falter. The dark liver gelding flew over the ground, his muscles straining as he moved from third place into second.

"Come on, Fred, move it!" Dylan shrieked.

Fred was beaten to the post by half a length.

"Second!" Malory cried.

Meg laughed and threw her arms around Henry.

Lani didn't take her eyes off Just Fred as his jockey rode him away from the track. Clancy hurried towards them, carrying a red and yellow striped blanket which he threw over Fred's quarters. Then he reached up to shake the jockey's hand.

"You've got it wrong, Lan," Honey murmured. "Someone's out to get Henry, but it's not Clancy."

Lani sighed. "But if not Clancy," she asked, "then who?"

Lani stared into the fire, mulling over the series of mishaps that had happened at Home Farm. An ember fell from the fire on to the hearth and flared for a moment on the brick before dying away.

Sam sat down opposite her. "As my gran would say, a penny for your thoughts."

Lani sighed. "I'd pay better money than that if someone could offer a solution to my thoughts."

Sam tilted his head and looked curious. "What is going on in there?" He reached over and gently tapped her forehead. "Are you determining the value of pi?"

Lani plucked at a loose thread on the fireside rug. "That would be easy by comparison. Doubt, suspicion and intrigue is what's going on in there," she said ruefully.

"Sounds like a Hollywood movie." Will headed into the room carrying a tray loaded with munchies. Behind him Dylan and Malory balanced glasses and a bottle of lemonade.

As they began to offload everything on to the low

coffee table, Honey popped her head around the door. "I've raided the DVD collection and it's a toss-up between *Mamma Mia* and *Quantum of Solace*."

"The film's on hold." Sam waved her in. "Lani's got something on her mind that's even more riveting."

Lani shook her head as the others joined her on the rug. Dylan passed around a bowl of crisps. "I bet it's got something to do with a slit girth," she guessed.

Sam and Will exchanged a bemused glance. "Slit girth?" Sam echoed.

"When we were carrying the tack out to the lorry this morning we found that Sweetie's girth had been cut with a knife," Malory told them.

Will's eyebrows shot up. "What did Henry say?"

"We didn't tell him," Honey admitted. "We figured he had enough on his mind today."

"I told Clancy," Lani said.

"What did he say?" Sam asked.

Lani shrugged. "He thanked me for letting him know."

"That was it?" Sam frowned. "Didn't he say that it would have to be reported to the police? I would have thought he'd have wanted to know where the girth was so he could hand it over as evidence."

There was a pause. Honey bit her lower lip and looked uncomfortable. "Tell them about the water bucket," she said.

"But I thought we'd discounted that," Lani responded. "Just Fred came in second so it's obvious Clancy didn't do anything."

"Yes, but you'd seen him and maybe that stopped him from giving Fred the water," Honey argued.

"Slow down, guys! There are people in the room who are feeling like they've missed a crucial part of the conversation," Dylan interrupted.

"Lani saw Clancy going into Fred's stable with a bucket of drinking water just before his race," Honey explained.

"So you're saying that it might be Clancy who is behind all of the recent disasters?" Malory checked.

Honey knelt up and began pouring lemonade into the glasses. "I think we're saying that we're not sure, but he might be."

"Sounds like you've got it all wrapped up." Will stretched out on the rug and put his hands behind his head. "Time to get the police involved, surely?"

"Wait, let's work through this logically," Lani said. "Things have happened at the yard that can't all be explained away as accidents, or," she glanced at Dylan, "an ancient curse. Before we got here Zhivago's Colonel had an accident out on the gallops and I Should Be So Lucky developed anaemia. Reg said it was part of a curse and, almost as if that gave someone an idea, other things started to go wrong that weren't accidents."

"The puppies were let out and the chicken run was opened when Daniel Blanchett came to inspect the yard," Dylan said, counting on her fingers. "The water buckets were tipped over. Barbed wire was stretched across the gallops, and Sweetie's girth was slit."

"Are you saying that Henry's upset someone and

they're out for revenge?" Will queried. "Because I can't think of any other reason for someone trying to sabotage him."

"I don't know the motive," Lani admitted. "But the perpetrator has to be someone on the yard. There's no way a stranger could have carried out all those things without being seen."

The door opened and Amy looked in on them. "Malory," she said with a smile, "Meg's just sent up a magazine for you from the Dower House."

"Great!" Malory jumped up. She crossed the room and took the magazine from Honey's aunt. "Thanks."

Heading back to the others, she explained, "Meg was telling me at the races about an article in one of her *Horse and Hound* magazines. It's about Amy Fleming coming to the UK to run a training course."

Sam sat up. "Ah, the famous wonder girl who fixes horses." He threw a peanut into the air and tried to catch it in his mouth.

"What is she, some sort of vet?" Will asked.

"She's training to be a vet," Malory told him, "but she works with horses who have emotional problems as well as physical."

Dylan looked over Malory's shoulder as she began to flick through the pages. "Stop!" she exclaimed. She jabbed her finger at a feature. "Where do I know him from?"

Lani peered over Malory's other shoulder. "He does look familiar," she said, looking at the portly man with ginger hair. He was pictured on an immaculate-looking yard standing between two glossy Thoroughbreds. Lani read out the caption: "Owner Julian Williams takes time out to show off his new racing yard."

Will grabbed up a handful of Sam's peanuts. "Julian Williams was at the party last Friday."

"It's the man who insulted your mum's Gainsborough!" Honey exclaimed.

"The one who tapped his nose every time he made a point," Lani recalled.

"The creep," Dylan added. "He's opening a yard?"

Malory skimmed the article. "It says he's in talks with several of the top owners in the business, including Daniel Blanchett."

Lani stood up and ran her hand through her hair. "I feel a major piece of the puzzle dropping into place. Julian Williams has set himself up as a rival trainer and is after the same owners as Henry."

"But he couldn't have arranged all of those things that went wrong," Honey pointed out. "He's never been to Home Farm."

"Yes, but he might be paying someone else to do it for him," Dylan said.

Lani sat back down on the rug and gave Dylan a high five. "Welcome to my wavelength."

"So, by making sure that Home Farm's reputation sucks, Julian gets to swipe his nearest competition's owners." Malory's dark blue eyes sparkled with indignation.

Lani nodded. "His yard becomes an overnight success, Henry's yard closes, job done."

"OK, so it's obvious to me that there's a simple solution to this," Will said. He left a deliberate dramatic pause as he joined in Sam's peanut-catching contest.

Dylan groaned. "Come on, come on, we're dying of suspense over here."

Will crunched on his peanuts before saying, "Dardanus is the favourite to win tomorrow. If he comes first, then the rumours about the Dysart Curse will lose a lot of credit."

"So we've got to make sure that nothing happens to stop Dardanus running well tomorrow." Honey sounded determined.

"But you know what else this means," Lani said, suddenly feeling cold. "It means that if Dardanus doesn't do well even more people will believe in the curse. The last thing owners will want is Henry training their horses."

Mrs Harper came into the room. "I hate to break up the party but you girls have got an early start in the morning."

"But Mum. . ." Honey protested.

"No buts." Mrs Harper held up her hand. "I'm sure whatever you were talking about can wait until tomorrow."

But that's just it, Lani thought with dismay. *Tomorrow may well be too late.*

Honey snapped on the bedside light. "I know we've got to be up early but I'm never going to sleep until we decide what we're going to do tomorrow."

"Ditto." Lani sat up in bed.

"How are we supposed to know what to do if we don't know what's going to happen?" Dylan pointed out, brushing a feather off her nose. "Honey, these pillows are leaking!"

Lani swung her legs off the bed. "Hang on," she said. "I'm going to go get the boys."

As she crept along the corridor to the boys' room, Lani suddenly stopped dead. A tiny memory had been flickering at the back of her mind, and the feather on Dylan's nose had jogged it free. *The man we saw with Clancy in Oxford was Julian Williams.* She was sure of it. The man had been of the same height and build, but more significantly, when he finished his conversation with Clancy outside the tearoom, he'd *tapped his nose.* It had to be Julian!

She rapped on the boys' door and slowly turned the handle. Sam and Will were sitting in the window seat playing a game of cards. "Lani!" Sam looked surprised to see her.

"Do you always burst into young gentlemen's rooms in the middle of the night when they are only half dressed?" The corners of Will's mouth twitched.

Lani put her hands on her hips. "First, I didn't 'burst'; second, it's not the middle of the night; third, I don't see any gentlemen, and fourth, you're not half—" She broke off as Will jumped up. "Oh, OK, you are half dressed." Her cheeks felt hot as she saw both Will and Sam were dressed in cut-off pyjama shorts and T-shirts.

Sam slipped off the seat. "Ignore my foolish cousin," he advised. "Is everything OK?"

"We were hoping you'd come and help us work out a plan of attack for tomorrow," Lani told him. She was dying to tell them that she'd seen Clancy and Julian Williams in Oxford but wanted to save it up for when they were all together.

"Sure we will," Sam agreed. "We were talking about it when you came in." He grabbed his dressing gown. "Let's go!"

Lani led the way back to the girls' bedroom. They all piled on to the four-poster bed and Lani held up her hand. "I'd ask for a drum roll but this is too serious."

"OK." Dylan shook back her hair. "You've got our attention. Shoot!"

"Do you remember we saw Clancy in Oxford?" Lani prompted. "Well, the guy he was with was Julian Williams!"

Honey's eyes widened. "Are you sure?"

"Totally," Lani promised. "One hundred per cent. Remember how he kept tapping his nose at the party, whenever he felt he'd made a point? Well, he did the same thing when he finished talking to Clancy in Oxford!"

Honey looked sad. "So it looks as if it is Clancy who's behind all of the attacks on the yard." She sighed. "I'm really sorry for not wanting to believe you yesterday."

"Don't sweat it," Lani told her. "I didn't want to believe it, either. Clancy seemed so nice when we first met him."

Will's voice hardened. "After everything Henry's done for Clancy, this is his payback? When Clancy started with Henry he knew nothing. Henry's spent a lot of time training him up for the top job on the yard. . ." He broke off, shaking his head in disgust.

"So what's our plan of attack?" Malory gave Will a sympathetic smile. "No one's going to believe Clancy's word against ours, so what do we do?"

"Simple," Dylan declared. "We just live up to our American rep. We make ourselves as interfering and nosy as possible!"

Lani grinned, catching on. "We follow Clancy everywhere, asking him questions about everything."

Malory tipped back her head and laughed. "He won't be able to breathe without us asking how it's done!"

Lani's smile died as Honey shook her head. "Guys, don't you see? If we stop Clancy from scuppering the race tomorrow he'll just do something next time when we're not here to stop him."

"So what are we supposed to do?" Sam demanded. "Stand back and let Clancy sabotage Henry again?"

Honey shook her head. "No, we give Clancy a chance to start what he's planning and we stop him in time for Henry to see what's going on."

Will let out a low whistle. "Talk about a risky strategy. What happens if we don't stop him in time?"

"The way I see it, we don't have a choice," Lani said, her heart sinking. "We just have to make sure that Clancy's caught. Which means hard evidence, right? Most of us have camera phones to record what happens."

Sam rubbed his hands over his face. "It's not a perfect plan but it's all we've got to work with." He held out his hand. "It's all going to boil down to teamwork."

Lani placed her hand on his. "Teamwork," she echoed.

One by one the others laid their hands on top. "To tomorrow," Dylan announced. "And the end of the Dysart Curse!"

Lani flicked a strand of white horse hair off her Albert Ferretti black trousers. All the girls had opted for trousers and flats, even though it was traditional to dress up for the Classic Cup. *But if we're going to be sneaking around after Clancy, skirts and heels aren't exactly going to cut it.*

"At least Clancy won't have had a chance to do anything to Dardanus this morning with everyone fussing around," Dylan murmured to Lani.

They looked into the temporary stable alongside the grey gelding's and were surprised to see Wayne tacking up Hazel. "I thought Hazel was one of Jess's horses?" Honey said.

"She is," Wayne puffed as he pulled up the girth. "But she's had car trouble today and hasn't been able to get in. She's coming straight down here as soon as it's sorted but she'll miss some of the races."

Lani swapped a dismayed glance with Malory. *What if Clancy did something to Jess's car to have one less pair of eyes watching him?* Her fingers tightened against her palms. *Well, there are four sets of eyes to replace hers.*

Clancy hurried up. "It's time for the first race," he said pointedly to the girls. "You'll have a better view from the stands." He looked at Wayne. "Is she ready?"

Wayne gently pulled Hazel's front leg forward to free any skin caught under the girth. "She's good to go."

"OK, you can take her down to the paddock. With Jess not here I need to keep an eye on Dardanus," Clancy told him.

Lani's mind went into overdrive. They had to stop Clancy being left alone with Dardanus. As she hesitated, Will and Sam walked down the lane of stables.

Thinking on her feet, Lani called, "Sam, you're late! We're going to be under pressure now to get this interview done."

"What int . . . Ow," Dylan said as Lani stepped heavily on her foot.

Apart from a slight frown, Sam played along. "Sorry, we got held up in the crowds."

Lani turned to Clancy. "Back at school we have a newspaper called *View from the Hill*. I've promised to write a feature for it all about the famous Dysart Racehorses. It wouldn't be complete without an interview with the head lad, or the photographs that Sam's going to take."

A light of understanding came into Sam's eyes as he took out the digital camera that Lani knew he'd brought along.

"It'll have to be another time," Clancy told her. "I've got to check on Dardanus."

Lani shook her head. "My deadline for emailing it is this evening. I really do need to do this interview with you now."

Honey interrupted them. "I know that Henry's really keen to help out the newspaper. I bet he wouldn't mind coming down to set you free to talk with Lani."

Lani held her breath, desperately hoping that Clancy wouldn't call their bluff.

An expression of annoyance flitted over the head lad's face. "There's no need for him to come down and miss Hazel's race. What do you need to know?" He looked around at them. "It doesn't take six of you to interview one person, does it?"

"We'll see you up in the owners' enclosure," Honey said quickly.

As the girls and Will left, Clancy raised an eyebrow. "Isn't it usual for a reporter to take notes?"

Lani hesitated as she desperately sought for a plausible reason for not having a notebook.

"Pen and paper's so over," Sam said in a decent imitation of an American drawl. "Lani's got an electronic voice recorder built into her phone."

With a tiny wave of gratitude, Lani fished out her phone and pretended to press a few buttons on her menu. "OK," she said. "We're all set." She flashed her brightest smile at Clancy. "How did you first become involved in the world of racing?"

Sam took shots on his camera as Lani pretended

to record Clancy's responses. Finally Clancy had had enough. He looked at his watch and declared, "That's it. I've got work to be getting on with." Without waiting for Lani's response, he headed into Dandy's stable.

Swapping a desperate glance at Sam, Lani kicked out and knocked over the grooming box outside the stable door. Clancy looked out, his eyebrows raised in surprise.

"Oh, I'm so clumsy!" Lani tapped her hand against her forehead. "Don't worry, I'll get it cleared up." She knew Clancy wouldn't dare do anything to Dardanus with her and Sam right outside the door. Slowly they restacked the brushes and tools back into the box.

The sound of hooves made Lani look up. The runners from the last race were being led back to their stables. "How did she do?" Lani asked Wayne as Clancy came out of the stable behind her.

"Fifth out of six." Wayne patted Hazel's damp neck. "I guess we're going to have to put it down to a bad day."

Lani glanced at Sam and read her own suspicion in his eyes.

Dardanus looked out over his door and gave a low whicker. Turning to see who the gelding was calling to, Lani saw Meg walking towards them with Henry. "I've come to wish Dardanus luck," she said. Meg dropped a kiss on the gelding's nose before gently stroking his cheek. Dardanus whiffled at her hair before pretending to chew it. "You are such a sweetheart!" Meg laughed as she straightened her hat. She smiled at Clancy. "How's our boy today?"

"Oh, he's just fine, Meg," Clancy replied. "A win's in the bag, I should say."

"I'm betting on it," Meg said mischievously. She turned to Lani and Sam. "Come on, you two. We're all having lunch in my box. The others are waiting for us."

Lani panicked. She had to find another excuse for staying near Dardanus. *He can't be left on his own until after he runs.*

Clancy glanced at his watch. "I should have been over with a friend's runners five minutes ago," he told Henry. "I promised to help get them ready for their races."

Lani felt relief wash over her.

Clancy called to Wayne. "You can take your lunch when I get back. I'll be away half an hour at the most."

I'll make sure that's all we're away for, too, Lani vowed.

They made slow progress along the tarmac lane leading to the members' enclosure. Crowds of smartly dressed spectators stood in groups chatting. Lani ducked to avoid being assaulted by a hat so large that the lady wearing it was almost lost from sight. "Killer ostrich feather at three o'clock," Lani murmured out of the side of her mouth to Sam.

Sam was distracted by the electronic board alongside the lane as it flashed up the odds for Classic Cup race. "Dardanus is coming in below Great Expectations at 9 to 2." He frowned. "I thought Dardanus was the favourite to win."

"He was." Henry's face looked creased with worry.

Meg waved her hand dismissively. "Those silly

rumours doing the rounds about the Dysart Curse have made some people doubtful about Dandy's performance. But our boy's going to show them all, you'll see. And the going's good to firm which is just how he likes it."

Lani crossed her fingers behind her back.

Henry led the way up to Meg's private viewing box, which had huge windows with spectacular views over the racecourse. "Wonderful, you're here!" Amy exclaimed. She raised a champagne flute. "We're waiting to raise a toast to success for Dardanus."

"Sparkling elderflower," Honey told Lani as she leaned across the table to hand her a glass.

Lani stood by her chair and raised her glass. "To Dardanus!"

As they took their seats, Dylan leaned closer to Lani and murmured, "I so loved your interview idea. Where's Clancy now?"

"He's gone to help get a friend's horses ready," Lani replied. "He's not going to be around Dardanus for the next half an hour."

Dylan's eyes widened. "How do we know he won't slip back to do something when you're not there?"

Lani felt sick. *Why didn't I think of that?* She turned to Sam. "I have to go back to the stables. Can you cover for me?"

"For a four-course meal?" Sam's eyebrows shot up. "I know my parents are caught up in the excitement of the big race but not so much that they won't notice you skip lunch."

"What happens if Clancy sneaks back to the stable while we're up here?" Lani hissed.

"Is everything all right?" Mrs Harper spoke from further up the table. She pulled off her long white gloves and laid them over the back of her chair.

"Fine," Sam said easily. "You look amazing, Mum, a definite shoo-in for Best Dressed Lady. How on earth do those ribbons manage to stay in that position?" Black and white ribbons stood stiffly out from Mrs Harper's hat.

Way to go with the distraction technique, Lani silently congratulated Sam.

Dylan nudged Lani. "Will says there are cameras out in the foyer where owners can check on the horses in the stables. We can take it in turns to go and watch them."

Lani pushed back her chair. "Um, excuse me, I just have to go to the bathroom."

She hurried out and found the row of television screens. Scanning them so fast that her eyes ached, she spotted Dardanus and Hazel looking out of their stables. Wayne was chatting with another stable lad further up the row. *Where's Clancy?* Lani wondered. She checked out the multiple screens and paused when she saw the familiar blond-haired lad carrying a set of tack into a stable. Satisfied that Clancy would be busy for a short time at least, Lani turned to head back to Meg's box. She took three steps and then stopped. Spinning around, she stared at the trainer's name that was chalked on the stable door where Clancy had just vanished.

"Julian Williams," she breathed. "Clancy's helping with Julian Williams' horses!"

She hurried back to the box and slipped back into her seat. A bowl of chilled avocado soup had been set in her place. Aware of her friends' eyes on her, she murmured to Dylan, "Clancy's in the middle of tacking up horses for Julian Williams!"

Dylan's eyes sparkled with surprised indignation. She turned to Will and whispered Lani's message. Will gave a small shake of his head before passing it on to Honey and Malory.

"Is there something wrong with the soup?" Lord Timothy asked.

Lani shook her head. "No, sir. It's absolutely delicious."

"And you can tell that just by its appearance?" Lord Timothy's lips twitched.

Feeling herself blush, Lani picked up her spoon and sipped some of the soup.

As the soup was cleared and plates of smoked salmon blinis, savoury éclairs and coronation chicken were put on the table, Honey stood up.

"Is this a game of musical chairs?" There was a hint of exasperation in Mrs Harper's voice.

"I won't be long," Honey said apologetically. "I just need to splash some water on my face. I feel really hot."

"Try running cold water over your wrists," Amy called after her. "It works for me every time."

"Oh my gosh! Check out that hat!" Dylan pointed at

a group of women chatting near the white post-and-rail fencing at the edge of the racetrack. One of the women was wearing a fuchsia hat which had two huge hoops attached to it. "It looks like a planet in orbit!"

"I'm sure that's Lady Louise's niece," Meg mused. She turned to Henry. "Do you remember? She came to see you for advice on which horse sales she should attend?"

Becky nudged Henry who looked up in surprise. "He's miles away," she explained to Meg.

"Sorry, Meg." Henry added his own apologies. "I don't think I'm going to be much use to anyone until this race is over."

Lani was distracted by Honey slipping back into her seat. "Everything's fine," Honey mouthed.

Lani could only pick at the food even though it was delicious. She glanced at her watch when the waiters came to clear the table.

"Don't fret. I'm on it," Sam murmured. He pushed back his chair. "Excuse me everyone. I'm just going to place a small bet."

Dylan sputtered with laughter as Meg said, "Do you know, I think my hearing's finally giving out on me. I could swear Sam just said he was going to place a bet!"

Cocktail glasses filled with meringue, strawberries and cream were set on the table. "Eton Mess," Mr Harper said appreciatively. "I can't remember the last time I had this."

A knot of tension was growing in Lani's stomach. *Sam should be back by now. What's the hold-up?*

Just as she was wondering what excuse she could

come up with to leave the table, Sam came back in. He bent over and whispered in Lani's ear, "It might be nothing but I've just watched Clancy hand over an apple to a young boy who's heading down the lane that Dandy's stable's in."

Lani leapt up. "We've got to check it out!" she gasped.

Sam matched her stride for stride as they raced out of the box and pounded across the foyer.

"What's the problem?" Dylan called from behind as she and the others raced after Sam and Lani.

"Might be trouble," Lani yelled, ignoring the raised eyebrows of a group of men in top hats and tails.

She and Sam took the stairs that led outside two at a time. Bursting into the sunshine, they pushed their way through the crowds. "This way!" Sam tugged at Lani's arm and steered her up a side alley. They vaulted a barrier and flashed their passes at the startled security guard before racing along the first row of stables. Lani dodged a stable lass and almost fell over an upturned bucket. Sam reached out and grabbed her arm to steady her. "OK?" he panted.

"Thanks." Lani only had enough breath for the one word as they put on a fresh spurt of speed and turned down the next row of stables.

"That's him!" Sam shouted, pointing at the boy standing outside Dandy's stall.

"Stop!" Lani bellowed.

The boy turned in surprise, his hand still outstretched with the apple on his palm.

Sam leaped and struck the apple out of the boy's hand.

"Gotcha," Lani said triumphantly, catching the apple in mid-air. "And," she added, glaring at the boy, "we've got you!"

Dardanus snorted in fright and skittered to the back of his stable.

"That hurt! What did you grab me for?" the boy demanded.

Lani softened. He could only be about seven. "You shouldn't have been giving Dardanus an apple," she told him.

Will skidded to a halt closely followed by Dylan, Malory and Honey. "What's going on?" Dylan demanded.

"We were just finding out," Sam panted. He turned to the boy. "Why did you choose Dardanus? Why didn't you give the apple to one of the other horses?"

"It was a good luck apple," the boy said. His lips quivered. "It was especially for D . . . Dardanus."

"Who said?" Lani asked gently.

The boy looked past her. "Him," he pointed.

Lani spun around. Clancy was at the end of the row of stables, a look of dismay on his face.

Will took the apple from Lani. "What's the betting there's an extra little something in here?"

"We've got him," Dylan said with a note of satisfaction.

"Moot point." Malory's voice rose in panic. "He's making a run for it!"

Lani suddenly felt a surge of anger. *There's no way he's going to get off the hook! He's going to face up to what he's done.* She grabbed a pushbike that was leaning against the opposite stable. Throwing her leg over the saddle, she pushed hard on the pedals, chasing through the yard after Clancy.

"Watch out!" one of the stable lads shouted as she almost mowed him down.

"He's a cheat!" Lani yelled. "Stop him!" Within moments she had caught up with Clancy. Turning sharply, she slammed on the brakes. Clancy tumbled over the front wheel and sprawled on to the ground.

The stable lad caught them up and pinned Clancy down. "What's he cheated at, then?"

"Not *what*, but *who*." Henry spoke grimly as he arrived behind them. "He's cheated me of my reputation."

Lani's legs suddenly felt wobbly. Setting the bike down, she was glad to hand things over to Henry. "Boy, am I glad you followed us," she said. "We think he was trying to dope Dardanus."

The others rushed up. "Wow, that was some fast thinking, Lani," Sam said admiringly.

"I was half expecting you to pull a lasso out of your

pocket and rope him." Despite her attempt at a joke, Dylan's voice sounded shaky.

Wayne hurried over. "What's going on?" He looked around in astonishment. "I got a phone call saying someone was trying to break into the horse lorry but it must have been a hoax because when I got there everything was fine."

Will handed the apple to Henry. "The core's been cut out and some white gloopy stuff's been pushed inside," he told him.

"We'll send it off for analysis." Henry stared down at Clancy and shook his head. "I just don't understand why you did it. You've worked harder than anyone to build up the yard."

The stable lad allowed Clancy to stand up but kept his hands pinned behind his back. Clancy spat on the ground and refused to meet Henry's eyes.

"We think he's working for Julian Williams," Honey said. "We can't prove he's involved, though."

"No, but it's something that the police will look into," Henry replied. His eyes glittered. "You're a fool, Clancy. You've thrown everything away, and for what? What was Williams prepared to pay you for ruining my name? I hope it's enough to support a change of career because you'll never work in this industry again." He took a deep breath. "Will?"

"Yes?" Will stepped forward.

"Go with Sam to get the Chief Steward of the Racecourse," Henry ordered. "And tell him to bring security."

Will and Sam hurried past Jess who was standing a short distance away, looking at them in bemusement. "What's going on? I've only just managed to get a lift here. I was going to go straight to help sort out the horses but. . ." Her voice trailed away as she gazed at Clancy. He was staring down at the ground, his blond hair hiding his face. "Clance?"

"We'll fill you in later but all you need to know right now is that you're my new head lad. Wayne, you're now travelling head lad, and I need you both to go and get Dardanus ready." Henry brushed off his hands on his jacket. "We've got a race to win!"

Lani squeezed in beside Honey and Sam and stared down at the racecourse. "How much tension overload do you think a person can take before they need to see a shrink?"

Sam grinned. "Oh, I'd say you're there already."

Lani dug him in the ribs. "Not funny." She hugged her arms to herself. She felt the same rush of nerves as before a major competition. *If Dardanus doesn't win, Henry might still lose everything.*

"There's Dardanus!" Malory exclaimed.

Turning her attention back to the racecourse, Lani homed in on the dappled grey as he cantered down to the starting line. Dardanus joined the circling horses, his coat flashing like a handful of pebbles among the glossy bays and chestnuts. The sun was shining strongly, reflecting off the grandstand's glass windows. Suddenly Lani wished she could be galloping along the bright green stretch of grass.

"Where are the stalls?" Dylan asked.

"They're using a starting line this time," Meg told her. "The horses will keep circling until the starter calls them forward, then the line will go up and off they'll go. It's important none of the horses make a break for it or we'll have a false start."

The buzz from the crowd below them rose on the air as suddenly the horses bounded forward at some invisible signal from the racecourse steward. *"And they're off!"* came the commentary over the loudspeaker. A chestnut and a bay broke away from the rest of the field. "And it's Great Expectations and Festival of Lights making a good getaway."

Lani's heart sank. Dardanus was a third of the way down the pack, caught in the press of horses struggling to find space to gallop after the busy start.

"Come on, Mike!" Henry called. "Get him out of there!"

Lani glanced at Meg and saw her face stretched taut with worry. "Move, Dardanus!" Meg's lips formed the words but no sound came out.

Lani looked back at the field, willing a space to open so that Dardanus could get free. On the other side of the rails, vehicles sped after the horses with video cameras pointed at them to record their progress.

"If he doesn't make his move soon, it's going to be too late." Henry's voice was brittle.

Lani gripped the balcony rail in front of her. "Come on, Dandy," she murmured. As the horses thundered around the track, Lani lost sight of the grey. *We can't have come this far for Dardanus to lose with the finishing post in sight.*

Suddenly there was a flash of pale grey. "He's making a break for it!" Dylan shrieked. With the horses beginning to tire and string out, a gap appeared and Mike crouched low and urged Dardanus away. With a spurt of speed, the grey lowered his head and began to extend his stride.

"And it's Dardanus suddenly deciding that there is a race to be won," announced the commentator. Lani gripped Sam's arm as Dardanus flew over the ground until he had drawn level with the bay. "And at the turn for home it's between the favourite Great Expectations, Festival of Lights, and Dardanus."

"He's second!" Honey cried as Dardanus pulled past the bay. "Come on, Dandy, you can do it!"

"Go, Dandy, go!" Lani jumped up and down.

Mike crouched low over the gelding's neck urging him on. Dandy's nostrils flared as he stretched out and found a final burst of speed.

The crowd began to roar as the horses drew closer to the finishing post. Great Expectations' jockey glanced back and saw Dandy's nose level with Great Expectations' tail. He swung his whip but Lani could see that the chestnut was beginning to tire. Her heart pounded as Dardanus edged level with Great Expectations. "We're inside the final furlong and they're neck and neck," said the tannoy.

"Just a little more," Malory urged as Dandy's muscles strained to carry him past Great Expectations.

As the horses flashed past the post, Lani didn't dare to believe that Dardanus had won it.

"And it's Dardanus by half a length!" came the announcement. Mike stood in his stirrups and punched the air victoriously.

Over the cheers and applause from the crowd, Lani cried, "He's won, he's won!" She threw her arms around Sam, who swung her around in a circle.

Henry's eyes glistened. "I thought for a moment back there that he wasn't going to do it," he said hoarsely. "I thought I was going to lose everything." He rubbed his hand over his face.

"Lose?" Meg challenged her nephew. "You may not have the Dysart name but you're a member of the family, and losing's not in our blood." She gave Becky a quick hug before offering her arm to Henry. "I believe we're wanted in the winners' enclosure!"

"Dardanus, ridden by Mike Anderson, owned by Lady Margaret Dysart and trained by Henry Stilling wins the Classic Cup," declared the commentator, sounding as pleased as if it was his own horse.

Lani turned to hug Honey. "This is fantastic!" she whooped.

Honey fanned her hand in front of her face. "I'm glad that's our last race of the day. I don't think my heart could stand much more!"

Linking arms, they looked down as Jess led Dardanus into the winners' enclosure. An interviewer walked beside them holding a microphone up to Mike while a backwards-trotting cameraman zoomed in on the jockey's face.

"We're going to go down and congratulate Mike. Do you want to come with us?" Mrs Harper called as the adults made a move to leave the box.

"Sure," Honey answered for them all.

By the time they made it down to the winners' enclosure, Dardanus was unsaddled. Jess threw a bucket of water over the gelding's steaming coat and then a rug was buckled over him with the word *Winner* emblazoned on the sides.

As everyone else crowded around Mike to congratulate him, Lani slipped over to say hi to Dardanus. She exchanged a smile with Jess before telling the gelding, "You did good today." Dardanus turned his large dark eyes on her and nudged her with his nose. "I know," Lani said with a laugh. "You're thinking, quit all this fuss already and let me go collapse in my stable." She patted his damp neck. "Enjoy your moment of glory," she whispered. "You won much more than a silver cup out there today."

"There were so many best moments today that I don't know which was my favourite," Dylan declared happily as she sat down at the dining table.

Will grinned. "It has to be Lani's Wild West on Wheels display."

"I'll be available to sign autographs at the end of the evening," Lani announced as she cut her slice of roast beef. "Although Best Moment trophy has to go to Dardanus being first past the post."

"Closely followed by Daniel Blanchett saying he

wanted to put his horses with you." Honey smiled across the table at Henry and Becky.

"I liked that moment too," Henry replied. "Although it wouldn't have happened if it hadn't been for all of you. Thank you." His voice was full of emotion as he looked around the table.

Amy broke in. "I feel as if you've all only just arrived. I can't believe you're flying home tomorrow. The house is going to seem so empty."

Lani felt a stab of longing for everything to stay the same. *How am I going to get on that plane knowing I'm leaving Honey and Sam behind?* She glanced at Sam and saw he was thinking along the same lines. Swallowing hard, she forced a smile. "You'll be so busy moving into your new house and starting school that you'll hardly notice we're gone."

"I'll notice," Sam said quietly.

"Didn't someone mention presents earlier?" Meg broke the sudden silence.

Honey pushed back her chair. She headed over to the sideboard where a small pile of gift-wrapped items had been placed on a silver tray. "We wanted to give each of you something to remember us by." She blinked hard as she carried the tray back to the table.

Don't cry, Lani begged silently. *I'm barely holding it together here.*

Mrs Harper handed Honey a tissue. "I came prepared," she murmured.

"Thanks, Mum." Honey swiped the tissue under her eyes before turning to Malory. "These are for you."

Malory carefully unwrapped a pair of leather riding gloves. "They're beautiful!" She stroked them with a look of awe on her face.

"We thought they were just the thing for your future A-Level circuit success," Honey explained. She handed Dylan the next parcel.

"It's a remote control for a futuristic transporter which means we can see each other at the touch of a button," Dylan guessed.

"I wish," Honey chuckled. "It's a video iPod which we've loaded up with footage from the ball and of us, as well as all of your favourite songs and some of ours. Blame Dad for the Beatles."

"Best of British," Mr Harper told her.

Honey rolled her eyes before handing Lani her gift. She sat down on the sofa beside Lani to watch her unwrap it.

"They're gorgeous." Tears blurred Lani's vision as she opened the blue velvet box and stared down at a pair of silver spurs engraved with the words, *Honey and Lani, BFF*. Lani reached over and hugged Honey. "Thank you so much," she whispered, not trusting her voice to speak out loud.

"And this is for you, too." Sam handed her a photo album.

Curiously Lani flipped the book open. On the first page was a photo of her, Dylan, Honey and Malory dressed up for their first school party in Seventh Grade. Lani felt a stab of nostalgia. *It feels like it was yesterday and aeons ago both at the same time*, she realized.

Turning the page, she looked down on a photograph of Sam in a hospital bed. *That was the day we first met.* She remembered how she had covered for Honey to sneak out of school to visit her twin in hospital. Sam had been so unwell after his leukemia had returned, and Honey had been desperate with worry. She and Lani had got into a lot of trouble for leaving without permission, but it had been worth it to see the twins reunited.

Lani turned to the last but one page of the album and smiled at the group photo taken at the homecoming ball. Just below it was a photo that pictured them standing around Dardanus with Henry and Meg holding a large silver cup between them.

"I'll treasure it always," she said softly. She wondered why the final page was empty. Her eyes strayed to Sam's writing on the back cover.

I've left the last page in the album free because it's waiting for the memories we're going to make together in the future. Love always, Sam. P.S. The heart knows no distance.

A tear rolled down Lani's cheek and she dashed it away. Holding out her hand to Sam, she said, "I'll make that a deal and shake on it. And since I always make good on my deals, then I guess this means I'll be seeing you again, Sam Harper."

"And I'll be seeing you, Lani Hernandez," he promised.

Impulsively, Lani reached out and put her arms around Honey and Sam, hugging them both close.

"Best Friends Forever, however far away I am?" she asked.

Two matching blonde heads nodded against hers. "Best Friends Forever," they agreed.